# Loki

**This book belongs to:**

SPELLS

# LOUIE STOWELL

# LoKi

## A BAD GOD'S GUIDE TO MAKING ENEMIES

WALKER
BOOKS

First published 2024 by Walker Books Ltd
87 Vauxhall Walk, London SE11 5HJ

2 4 6 8 10 9 7 5 3 1

© 2024 Louie Stowell

The right of Louie Stowell to be identified
as author of this work has been asserted in
accordance with the Copyright, Designs
and Patents Act 1988

This book has been typeset in Autumn Voyage, Avenir,
Bembo, Blackout, Cabazon, ITC American Typewriter,
Liquid Embrace, Neato Serif, Open Sans, Times and WB Loki

Printed and bound by CPI Group (UK) Ltd, Croydon CR0 4YY

British Library Cataloguing in Publication Data:
a catalogue record for this book is available
from the British Library

ISBN 978-1-5295-1580-0
Exclusive edition 978-1-5295-2743-8

www.walker.co.uk

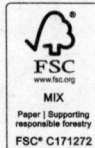

WALKER
BOOKS

FSC
www.fsc.org
MIX
Paper | Supporting
responsible forestry
FSC® C171272

To my mum

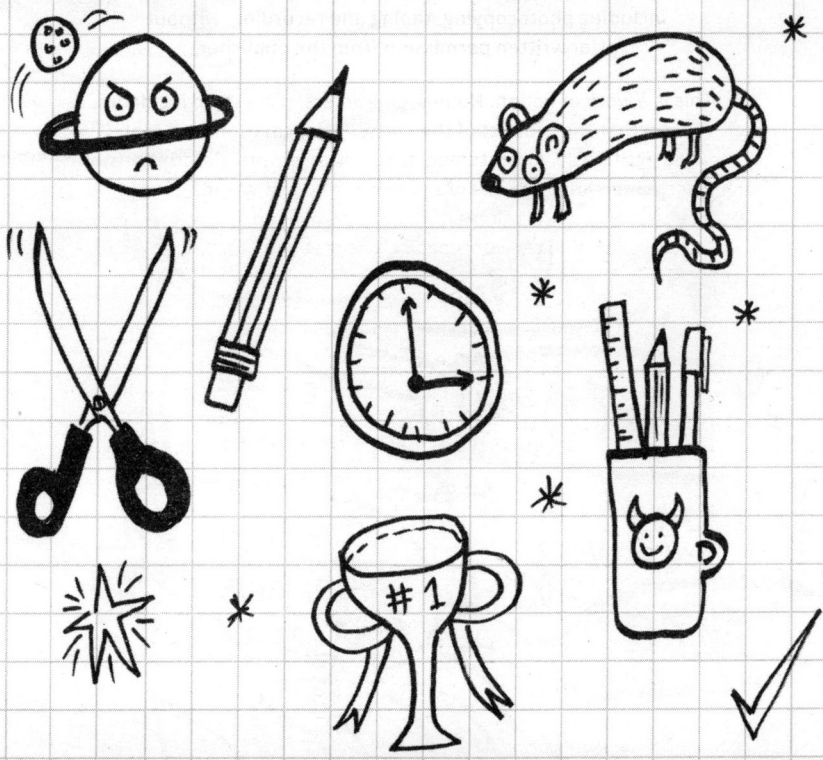

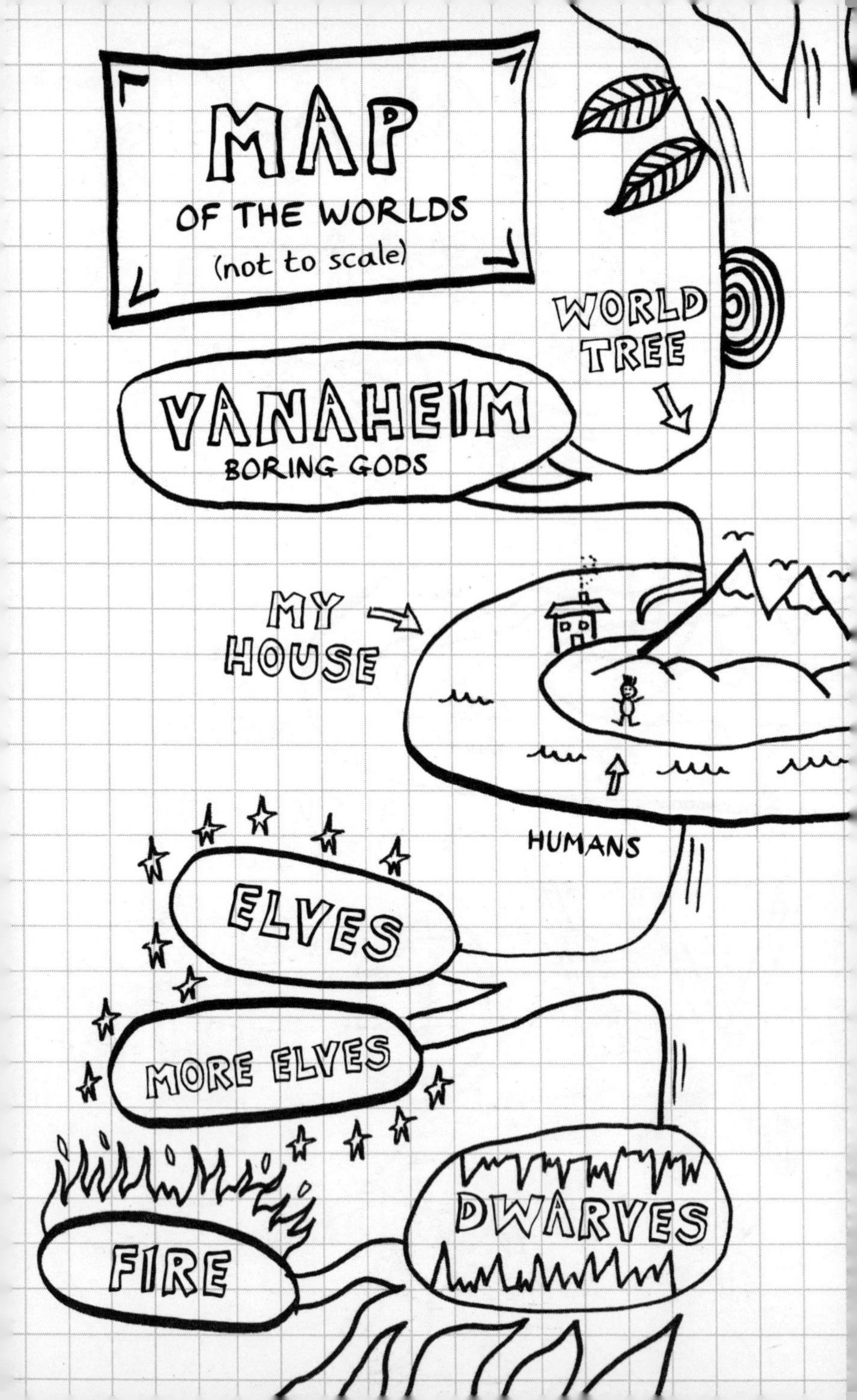

# MAP
## OF THE WORLDS
(not to scale)

WORLD TREE ↓

VANAHEIM
BORING GODS

MY HOUSE →

HUMANS
↑

ELVES

MORE ELVES

FIRE

DWARVES

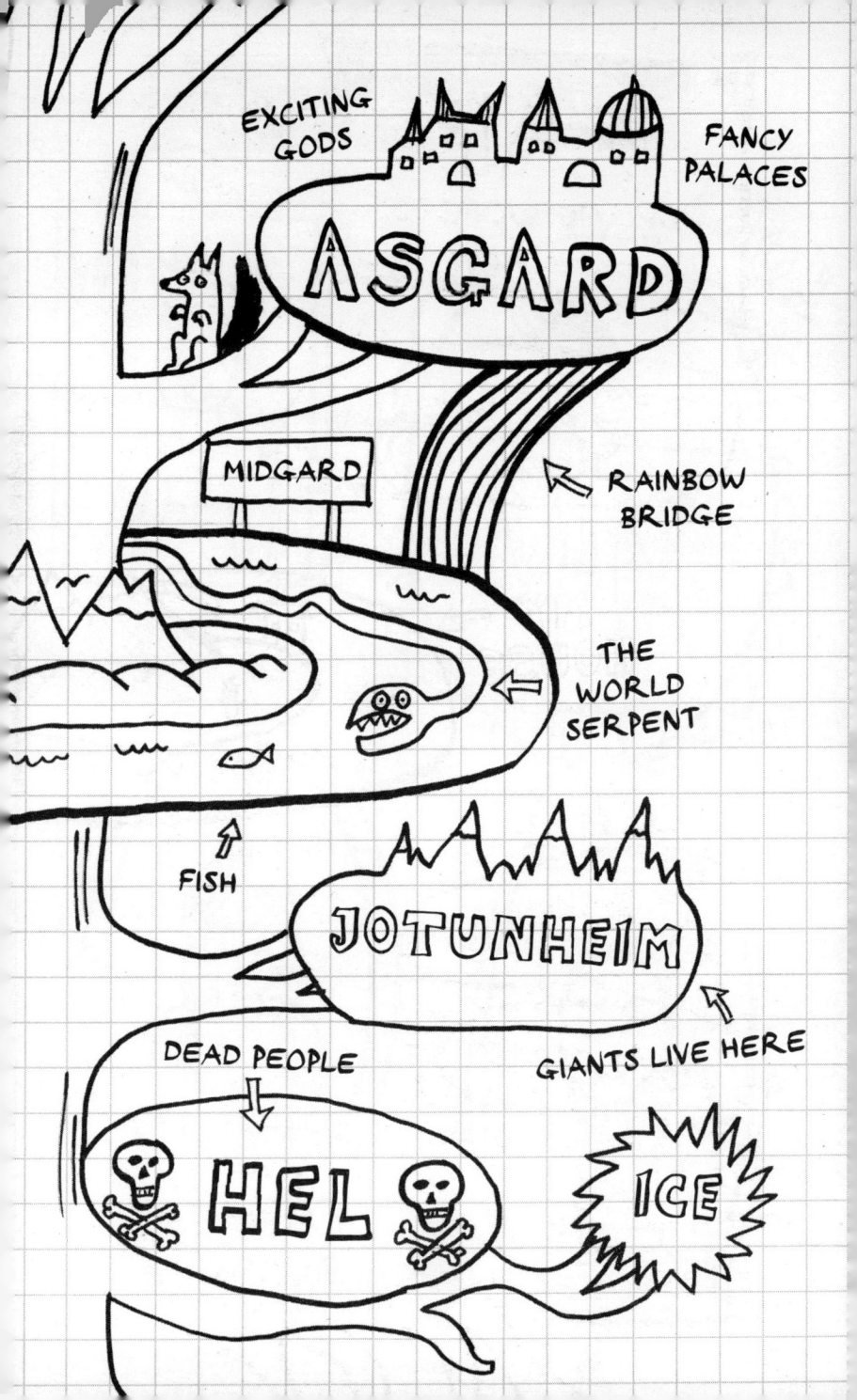

# The Characters

LOKI

THOR

GEORGINA

VALERIE

FIDO

HEIMDALL

HYRROKKIN

VINIR

ODIN

RATATOSK

# Timetable

| | | Monday | Tuesday |
|---|---|---|---|
| 1 | | MATHS | MATHS |
| 2 | | ART | HAND-WRITING |
| 3 | | SPELLING | ENGLISH |
| 4 | | TOPIC | GEOGRAPHY |
| 5 | | PE | SCIENCE |

LOKI vs LUNCH BREAK

I'm back, mortals! Miss me? Of course you did! How you must have suffered!

# About this book:

I am Loki, the Norse trickster god. Here are some important facts about me:

- I am currently in the form of a mortal boy
- I am a shape-shifter
- I was a horse once
- I am an expert magician

**Expert magician? Incompetent, arrogant beginner more like!** !

I must record my deeds on Midgard – what you might call Earth – in this magical diary, which corrects me when I lie.

Allow me to refresh your foggy mortal memories about some of my glorious adventures...

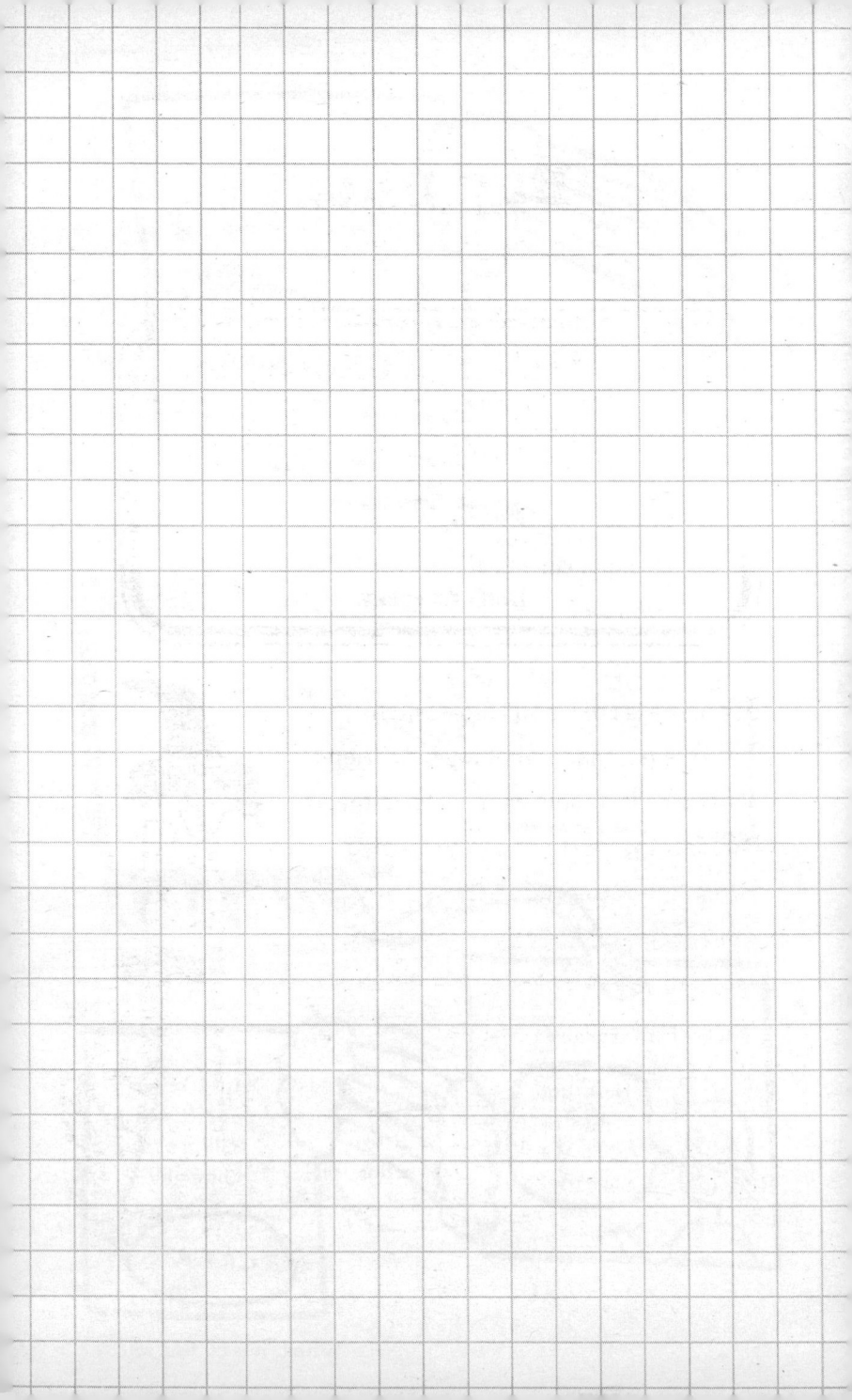

# **Day One:**
## Tuesday

My name is Loki, and I am a witch.

At least, that's what my best friend Valerie calls people who perform magic. Apparently, mortals used to burn witches, but they don't do that any more. I am not entirely sure why they stopped but Valerie says that open fires are bad for the environment, so maybe that is why.

*Oi! This is a low emissions zone, sunshine!*

CRACKLE

CRACKLE

As an extremely talented and handsome god, whenever I try something new I am immediately perfect at it. Which means I am already the greatest magician in history.

> **Do you need me to correct those shameless falsehoods, or shall I just clear my non-existent throat in a sarcastic manner?**

Agree to disagree. But, while I am a mighty wielder of spells, I will admit that, today, *one* of my spells went less than smoothly.

It all began at Breakfast Club...

**Breakfast Club:** a concept beyond space and time, where one is both at school and yet not. Also there is breakfast.

Valerie wasn't there that day so, while Thor went to find his sports friends, I sat with Georgina, and – more's the pity – her snot-ridden younger brothers.

Snot rag

Snot bags

"Oh hi, Liam," Georgina said. "Could you do me a favour and sit with David and Isaac while I go and get another jug of water?"

I acquiesced, with good grace.

Lie detected. You said, "If I have to." !

But I helped!

"What happened?" gasped Georgina.

"He *licked* my toast. HE LICKED IT!" wailed the smaller child.

"I helped reduce the excess butter! I'm good now!" I said.

"*Good?!* You think this is 'good'?" Georgina gave me a look of such scorn I am surprised the skin did not wither from my face. "You wouldn't know good if a choir of angels sang you the definition from the dictionary." She hastily bundled her brothers away from the table. "In fact," Georgina said, scowling over her shoulder, "I don't think you've ever done *anything* good for me the entire time I've known you."

I haven't?

Well, if Georgina wants good, I'll show her good...

In fact, I wasn't just going to show her good, I was going to show her...

FABULOUS

! I dread to ask what happened next.

In my quest to prove myself to Georgina, I told her to meet me in Ms Loach's classroom just before her class had their drama lesson. After an expression of great scepticism, Georgina agreed. Before her arrival, I blew up balloons and made a banner.

☆ GEORGINA IS THE BEST! ☆
LOVE FROM LIAM, HER DEAR FRIEND.

To truly make my gesture grand, I found a spell involving a shiny pebble. I hadn't practised it, but the spell was so easy that it posed no challenge for Loki, the cleverest of the gods...

**Oh. Oh no. Oh no no no.**                              !

Just as Georgina arrived in the classroom, I kissed the pebble to complete the spell. Glitter filled the air. For a moment, I saw my friend's eyes shine in delight...

WOW!

Pebble

Until the glitter turned to fire, and delight turned to fear, and the room erupted into chaos.

! That's actually worse than I was picturing.

Perhaps it would have worked out if the drama teacher hadn't swung the door open wearing a neon fire marshal vest, and seen the two of us standing soaked beneath a charred and soggy banner with both our names emblazoned on the cloth.

Upon seeing the remnants of my flaming handiwork, Ms Loach pointed to the fire exit, a fierce look upon her face.

"We must evacuate the building immediately. But after that – Georgina, Liam – once the building is safe you will go straight to the head teacher's office!"

"But, Ms Loach—" began Georgina.

"I don't want to hear it!" said Ms Loach. "With Liam, this feels standard. But Georgina? Arson?" She shook her head. "I am so disappointed."

Georgina's eyes glistened with furious tears. Or possibly sad tears.

I heard my conscience whispering.

> You need to take responsibility and get Georgina out of trouble.

Frustratingly ambiguous tears

This was my chance! To turn those (possibly) furious tears to smiles of joy and gratitude, and prove to Georgina that I AM good!

Ms Loach, Georgina didn't—

Evacuate. The. Building. Now!

Her eyes flashed with a fire as fierce as
the breath of the dragon Nidhogg. Her lips
curled in a snarl as cruel as the jaws of the giant
wolf, Sköll, who seeks to devour the sun!
Her fists shook with a rage as mighty as...

> ! **All right, all right, we get the idea. Stop
> hamming it up. She's just a teacher.**

*Just* a teacher? You are a sentient book. You can
have no concept of how terrifying a teacher can be to
one in the form of a mortal child!

Although Georgina and I had to stand in separate
groups in the playground because we are in different
classes, we were reunited as we walked to the head
teacher's office.

DOOM ➡

As Georgina and I walked swiftly along the
corridor, she said, "I can't believe you didn't admit it
was you! No, wait, I *can* believe it. You're the WORST!"

> She wouldn't let
> me speak!

24

25

The head teacher's office is a place I frequent as often as Thor breaks wind, but the way Georgina looked around as we entered, it was as if she were viewing the terrible mysteries of the Norns, who govern all our fates and yet will not disclose them.

Before I could explain that Georgina was innocent – and, more importantly, that I am a very good friend – the head held up his finger.

"Ms Loach informed me of your involvement in setting off the fire alarm," he said.

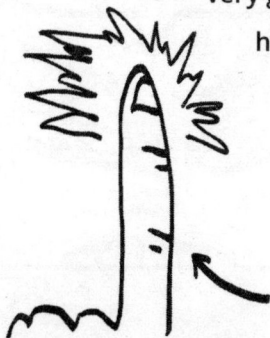

Universal signal for silence — none shall break this law

"Actually—" I began, only to be silenced by a glare more threatening than the battle rage of a whole cavalcade of Valkyries.

The head turned to Georgina. "I would expect better of you, Georgina Olowo. You're usually such a credit to this school. Your parents will be so disappointed."

Georgina shrivelled at that, like a sad slug under a mountain of salt.

"But sir..." I began.

"ENOUGH. Liam Smith, I have run out of ways to explain the consequences of your actions to you." The head teacher sighed deeply. "I will decide on your punishment shortly. Back to your classes, both of you."

He pointed to the door and we slunk out of the room like Fido does when Hyrrokkin catches him licking the furniture.

Before I could say anything to Georgina, she stalked off to her classroom, not looking back.

"Georgina, wait, I can fix this!" I called after her. But there was no point. For, as yet, I had no idea how.

# Day Two:
## Wednesday

## LOKI VIRTUE SCORE OR LVS:

# -250

**250 points lost for getting Georgina into trouble. Even when your heart is vaguely in the right place you still make moral missteps.**

When I met Valerie in the playground before school, I told her that Georgina had not replied to any of my text messages.

Have you been kidnapped by Frost Giants?

Have you drowned in the snot that emanates from the nasal cavities of your siblings?

Did an asteroid hit your house in the night?

Are you dead?

Valerie informed me that Georgina's parents had confiscated her phone. Of course! She had not seen my messages! That was the only plausible reason for not having replied!

> ## Is it?                                                    !

But as I made for the doors, declaring that I would speak to her before lessons, Valerie held me back.

"Don't," she said. "Georgina *really* doesn't want to talk to you."

This was most puzzling. "How do I fix things if I am not allowed to talk to her?" I perked up. "Perhaps another grand gesture?"

Valerie took my arm and led me to a quiet corner by the bins.

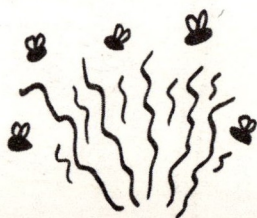

"Maybe leave Georgina alone for a while. Every time you talk to her, you seem to make it worse. I wish you'd stop being so—"

Before she could complete that no-doubt-unfair sentence, a ray of light beamed down from the sky and sucked me up into the air.

Aliens!

I closed my eyes tightly, as though not seeing my fate would make it go away. When I opened them, I was sitting on the floor in a blank glowing space; a tall, thin figure lurked in the shadows nearby.

Was it ... could it be ... was Valerie right? Was this...

"... an alien?" I said in disbelief.

"I thought a *god* would know. I am no alien." The tall, thin figure stepped out of the shadows.

30

I am Vinir Volundsson, a prince of Alfheim, a lord of the dark elves, son of the legendary smith, Volund!

The elf fixed his blazing eyes upon me and I shivered. There was rage in those eyes, and it appeared to be aimed at ME.

I have travelled long, from Alfheim to the depths of Hel itself, from frozen Jotunheim to lofty Asgard until, after many months, I discovered your hiding place in this meagre realm!

Months? You're not very good at looking, are you?

Vinir flung out his arms and declared, "I am here to wreak terrible revenge upon mine enemy!"

Then he looked pointedly at me.

"I'm sorry but ... who *are* you? Vinir ... who?"

The elf looked at me with disbelief. "Vinir Volundsson! Your mortal and most deadly enemy!"

I shrugged, drawing a blank.

The elf shook off his disappointment with a toss of his long silky hair and cleared his throat.

"Odin informed me you are a magic user and as such" – Vinir drew himself up so high he was practically standing on the tips of his exquisitely stylish boots – "I am here to challenge you to a magical duel to the death."

32

I swear he has fangs too!

"And ... why?" Honestly, I was stumped. Also I was not a fan of "to the death".

"I must satisfy my honour after you insulted me in front of my father at a party."

"You're going to have to narrow it down," I told him. "I have insulted a lot of people, at a lot of parties, in front of a lot of people's fathers."

It was at a feast in Freyja's hall. The feast on the night that you cut off Sif's hair.

"SNIP"

SNIP

Ohhh, that feast.

While I remembered the feast that had led to me being exiled to Midgard, I did not recall an elf. I'd had more important things to focus on.

"Your insults still ring in my ears, churl!" Vinir scowled. "The look of pity and disgust on my father's face..." He trailed off with a hiss of pain. "Our family live by a strict code of honour, as do all elves of the Court. An insult must be answered!"

GRRR

"You're seeking revenge because I called you names in front of Daddy?" I said. "Is that not a tad oversensitive? I mean, who cares what your dad thinks? Sounds like a boring loser to me if he can't take a joke."

This was (it transpired) the wrong thing to say, given that the elf grabbed me and slammed me against the wall of his magical vehicle with considerable violence.

WE WILL DUEL AT MIDNIGHT, FOUL FIEND! BRING YOUR WAND!

He let go, put away his wand and dusted off his hands as though he had touched something unclean.

It was time for some quick thinking.

I know little of the elves beyond the fact that they are very tall, annoyingly beautiful and adept at magic.

On the whole, elves and gods only tend to mix at feasts or other formal occasions. Very few gods have many in-depth dealings with their kind: Freyja, who taught them magic, just as she taught Odin; and Freyja's brother, Frey, who accidentally received one of the elven realms as a present. (Long story ... that I never listened to because Frey can't tell a tale to save his life.)

*I wanted socks!*

No. To evade this duel I had to work with what knowledge I *did* have, which was that this particular elf *really* cared about looking good in front of his father.

Pride and fear ...  →    ... when talking about his father

How could I use that to my advantage?

"We cannot duel," I said, alighting upon the perfect answer. "I fear it would bring you shame and your father would be SO disappointed."

"Shame? How so?" Vinir was suspicious, yet clearly a little nervous at the idea of disappointing his father.

"It is dishonourable to duel with someone half your size. In my mortal form, I am a mere child!" I said. "And you're, what? Seven feet tall? Your father would think it ridiculous!"

Vinir got his wand out again and pointed threateningly in my direction.

Then turn back into your true divine form, you coward!

I shook my head. "So sorry, but Odin has forbidden that I take on my godly form. Surely you are not suggesting I dishonour such a noble personage as Odin Allfather?"

! You dishonour him all the time!

And? Vinir didn't know that.

The elf's face went like this:

Eventually, with a growling sigh of defeat, Vinir gave in.

"Honour dictates I cannot bid you to disrespect Odin, nor can I duel with a child." His large eyes bored into me – if looks could kill, I would have been a smoking hole in the floor. "It appears you have thwarted my revenge."

I did an admirable job of looking repentant.

"Fine." Vinir's eyes flashed and he waved his wand at me in a way I did not like. "But this is not over."

People always say that when they're beaten but don't want to admit it.

He ignored that and sent me back in his glowing magical beam to where Valerie was waiting, her eyes as huge as plates at a feast. "Tell. Me. Everything."

"I mean ... weren't you worried about me?" I asked.

"Worried?" said Valerie. "I'm green with envy."

"But I just got kidnapped!" I objected.

"Not kidnapped." She held up a finger. *"Abducted.* You got abducted by ALIENS! My dream come true!"

**TELL ME EVERY DETAIL!**

As it turned out, Valerie didn't mind discovering that what she thought had been an alien was, in fact, an elf. Nor did she seem to mind that this elf had beamed me onto his chariot in order to kill me, such was her fascination with the alien/elf connection. Instead she scribbled furiously in her notebook.

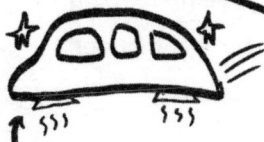

Elf chariots fly and look like this so people assumed they were alien UFOs.

This mistake is convenient to elves so they encourage it.

It seems aliens are a conspiracy theory to cover up elves! AWESOME!

"I can't believe you're so happy about elves,"
I sniffed. "This elf wanted to kill me!"

Valerie frowned. "Oh yes. Sorry. I got carried
away. Are you OK?"

OK? I am
WONDERFUL!

"For I defeated a foe without lifting a
finger, simply using my considerable wits!"

"You really think he'll just give up like that?"

"Of course!" I said. "He was utterly convinced
by my argument!"

"Hmm," said Valerie, the doubter.

I second that "Hmm" and would add a
"Not likely, Loki."

Sceptical
face

RUDE!

# Day Three:
## Thursday

### LOKI VIRTUE SCORE OR LVS:

# -250

#### Holding steady. For now.

In assembly, the head announced that we were having a school winter fair.

**School Fair:** an event where a school is turned into a place of commerce. The parents of the children who attend the school are strong-armed into helping, except in the cases of adults whose lives are so empty that they volunteer willingly.

The theme of the fair was to be Winter Wonderland. Since winter was coming to this mortal region, the theme was hardly original.

Tedious.

Now I am usually in favour of events that distract teachers from their day-to-day focus of inflicting misery in the form of lessons. But the winter fair was to be the harbinger of my DOOM.

**Oh?**                                                                 **!**

Patience, Diary. I'll get there.

"What's wrong?" I asked, ignoring the way Valerie was frantically waving her arms as if to waft me away.

"You," said Georgina. "My parents are SO angry with me. No – worse – they're *disappointed*."

I did not see how that was worse, but she continued.

"I'm *never* in trouble. They didn't believe I'd done it, so they made an appointment with the head to defend me and ask for evidence, but he showed them that stupid banner with my name on."

"And mine!" I said, not wanting to be left out.

Georgina glared at me. "They think I've done something terrible because of *you*."

I tried to think of something comforting to say but could not think of anything. So, to lighten her mood, I changed the subject. To *me*, the most fascinating subject of all. "Did Valerie tell you what happened to me yesterday?"

"She did. Tell me, Loki..." Georgina leaned forward and I felt cheered that she was showing such interest in this new topic of conversation.

Exactly how many people are going to come to Earth and seek revenge against you?

"What do you mean?" My good cheer began to melt like a Frost Giant lost in Muspelheim, the realm of fire.

Valerie got out her book and noted that down.

"How do you miss the point every single time?" said Georgina. "What I'm saying is: start treating people better before you upset someone competent enough to succeed in their revenge."

I scowled. "I do treat people well! I'm GOOD!"

At that, Georgina burst out laughing so hard I feared she might wet herself.

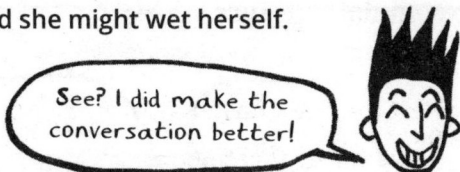

See? I did make the conversation better!

! I... But... Never mind.

Later, Georgina and I were summoned to the head's office to be informed of our punishment: attending detention after school twice a week.

During detention, you have to make decorations for the winter fair.

Georgina did not take the news of her first ever detention well.

BARF!

AAAH

44

**Correction: she muttered a bad word so mild that you could print it in a book for children and get no complaint letters.** !

When we left the headmaster's office, I said, "At least we will be together for the punishment. Even if detention is akin to a painful eternity of snake torture."

*She said BUMCAKES!*

*I would rather spend the rest of my life being torn apart by rabid dogs than spend A SECOND longer with you!*

After that I found myself feeling rather gloomy at the prospect of sharing detentions with Georgina.

**Could that be because it will be a constant, mortifying reminder of your inability to make people like you?** !

*HARSH, Diary. I'm going to bed to have a cry.*

**Sorry. Now I feel bad.** !

# Day Four:
## Friday

LOKI VIRTUE SCORE OR LVS:

# -150

**Plus 100 points because I feel bad about making you weep yesterday.**

At school, Thor did something ridiculous. Something that defies belief and leads me to wonder if, instead of being the God of Thunder, he is the God of Folly.

He *volunteered* to help at the school fair. Voluntarily! But when I discovered what he was volunteering for, it all made sense. He was offering to run the "score a goal against the goalie" stall for the sports teacher. Which means he will stand in the goal while people kick balls at him. Anything that involves kicking balls is one of his truest sources of joy in this mortal plane. I suspect that when we finally return to

Asgard he will try to introduce various sportsballs
to the gods.

SPIN

Let us do sports, Asgardians!

At break, I told him how ridiculous I found him.

"I cannot believe you are willingly participating
in this farce! Traitor! Do you not know that I am
suffering horrors for this cursed school fair?"

"It's not my fault that you did a bad thing and are
being punished while I find wholesome and useful
things fun," said Thor.

One sad consequence of my quest to become a
better person is that insults appear less readily on
my tongue. He was already walking away to join a
game of sportsball when I called after him.

You're a
stinky bum
bum head!

Concerned at such a feeble comeback, I decided to practise my insults on some of my classmates.

I don't care! My honour as the wittiest, cattiest of the gods is at stake here!

After school, Heimdall and Hyrrokkin were sitting in the living room, each on their phone. This was unusual. Heimdall doesn't use his phone during "family time" because his parenting books tell him that phones are basically a form of demon that will corrupt your soul and those of your children.

HEH
HEH
HEH

Hyrrokkin rarely uses her phone at all, except for the family group chat, or to search for new and unusual evening classes.

Search Classes that are violent but also creative

Kickbox sculpture class 

Interpretative dance mugging lessons 

Bare knuckle film criticism 

I glanced at my phone, praying to Odin that Balder the Perfectly Beautiful and Annoying had not messaged the family saying he was coming back to torture me with his self-righteousness and beautifully square jawline. Luckily he had not.

When Heimdall went to the loo, and Hyrrokkin was absorbed in her phone, I transformed into a moth and settled on the arm of the sofa where Heimdall had left his phone so I could read his screen.

49

**WINTER FAIR GROUP CHAT [45 people]**

PARENT WITH BROWN HAIR WHOSE NAME I NEVER CAUGHT
AND IT IS TOO EMBARRASSING TO ASK NOW:

Hi all, thank you for joining the winter fair committee,
please volunteer for a job from the list I shared earlier.

OVERLY ENTHUSIASTIC FATHER WHO RUNS THE BOOKSHOP:

Wonderful! I'll make my signature spelt biscuits!

MOTHER OF THE COATED ONE:

I'll run a face-painting stall. I can only paint butterflies.
If I make them blue would that be wintry enough?

PARENT WITH BROWN HAIR WHOSE NAME I NEVER CAUGHT
AND IT IS TOO EMBARRASSING TO ASK NOW:

And thanks to Kris and Elsa for suggesting
the fair theme! It's perfect!

UNKNOWN NUMBER:

Hello, it is Kris here.

UNKNOWN NUMBER:

Hi it is Elsa. Hello everyone.

HYRROKKIN:

I did not volunteer for this farce and I do not wish to be
involved. Even the theme is pathetic. Winter? What do you
know of winter? And how did any of you get my number?

At that dramatic point, I was interrupted by
Heimdall returning. Remaining in moth form, I
perched on his shoulder to read on. This was JUICY!
He started typing...

HEIMDALL:
Er, darling, I think you sent that to the whole group...

HYRROKKIN:
I know.

HEIMDALL:
Perhaps we should discuss this offline.

HYRROKKIN:
They all deserve to know that this is a foolish
waste of time and I am not ashamed to say it!

Heimdall started frantically messaging
the group saying that his wife was joking and
of course they would be overjoyed to help in
any way they could. They were both very delighted
and excited and flattered to be included ...

HEH
HEH
HEH

... which is how they are now charged with
several onerous tasks and must attend regular

meetings with the other tedious mortal
volunteers.

HA! I am not alone
in my punishment.

Over dinner, Hyrrokkin muttered about setting her
pet snakes on whoever gave those parents her number.

MUTTER
MUTTER
THREAT
THREAT

GULP

Hands trembling
with rage

Hands trembling
with fear

# Day Five:
## Saturday

## LOKI VIRTUE SCORE OR LVS:

# -250

**100 points lost for wilfully causing suffering to prove your verbal skills have not atrophied.**

*Worth it!*

The next morning, Hyrrokkin's anger had abated enough for her to propose a trip to the seaside, but not enough for me to refuse said trip. At least, not if I wanted to keep all my limbs. The weather was chilly and damp, but this did not put her off. Hyrrokkin is from Jotunheim, the icy land of the giants, where the temperatures fall below what mortals call "freezing" on even the balmiest days.

*Sigh! Gorgeous day!*

Hyrrokkin is not a Frost Giant herself, but the so-called winter weather in this part of Midgard feels like high summer to her. She even insisted we cover our exposed skin in the gloopy substance mortals call sunscreen.

COME HERE OR THE FIERCE RAYS OF THE SUN WILL FRY YOU!

I can't feel my fingers.

Thor and Heimdall seemed equally enthusiastic about the beach trip, but perhaps they just wanted to keep on her good side.

Even more enthusiastic (but in dog form Fido is enthusiastic about everything except bathing)

In order to reach our seaside destination, we were to take the train. This meant we needed to consult something called a train timetable.

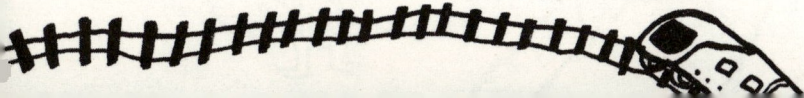

**Train Timetable:** a series of unreliable prophecies about when a train may or may not appear.

Public transport is a mortal notion I do not care for. Why should I share my chariot with the unwashed masses rather than drive in comfort? When I asked this loudly on the train, Hyrrokkin shushed me.

> It's better for the environment. And it's faster. And please keep your voice down.

After a tedious journey involving a lengthy lecture from Hyrrokkin about global warming and using my inside voice, we arrived at the seaside to be greeted with a blast of icy wind.

> Ah, the balmy sea air!

SHIVER

When we got down to the beach, we made a sandcastle.

KNOCK KNOCK

**!** I believe you are confusing the words "we" and "they".

Then we ate food on the beach, which meant our food was full of sand. It seems mortals find this manner of eating novel and charming. I just found it gritty.

Cake à la grit

Sand-wich

I didn't know sand could get inside a banana, but it can!

Hyrrokkin and Heimdall then lay down on towels to read. This gave me and Thor a chance to explore. Thor threw a ball for Fido to bring back. Fido brought it back. They repeated this while I wandered down the vast expanse of the deserted beach, until I smelled something delicious. Since my gritty food had been most unsatisfactory, I followed the smell to a fish and chip shop on the seafront and witnessed a number of seagulls dive-bombing a young couple eating chips. This gave me an idea.

Nooo!

Thief!

By the time I had stolen chips from a number of unsuspecting mortals, it was time to go home. Not a bad day, in the end. For me. (If you were one of the people whose chips I stole, perhaps it was.)

# Day Six:
## Sunday

**LOKI VIRTUE SCORE OR LVS:**

# -750

Minus 500 points for seagull chip theft. Honestly,
Loki, you must know that's wrong by now, don't you?

Heimdall insisted on *more* "family time" today. In this
part of Midgard, it is an important mortal ritual to
spend Sundays trapped with your most annoying
kin. Since this requires an accompanying meal, we
were forced to aid him in the kitchen chopping
vegetables and peeling potatoes.

Well, I was forced. Thor did it willingly,
the sucker. He appears not to care that he
is being forced into child labour. Thor did
not agree.

Help!

You are thousands
of years old. This is
not child labour.

58

"Just because I've lived for eons, it doesn't mean I do not have rights! My body is still puny and vulnerable to fatigue like that of a child!"

"Don't hold the peeler like that," said Hyrrokkin. "You might lose a finger. And I don't think Odin would be very happy about growing you a new one – he's very busy seeking out prophecies at the moment."

Odin is always so tedious about prophecies. Personally I have no intention of letting the universe plan my destiny for me. I am Loki, God of Chaos! I shape my own destiny!

AND DON'T WE KNOW IT!

Norns, who govern all our fates. Allegedly.

Thor looked wistful at the mention of his father.

"Do you think he'll come and tell us about the prophecies he finds?" he asked.

"Probably not," said Heimdall. "He likes to keep his prophetic cards close to his chest. Only after a lot of mead did he tell me about Fimbulwinter – the terrible winter that will come before Ragnarok."

Hyrrokkin snorted. "Winter? As though that's something to be afraid of. Bring it on!"

"But Hyrrokkin, the end of the world follows on from Fimbulwinter!" said Heimdall.

I try not to let apocalyptic prophecies bother me. None of them have come true as yet.

After all the vegetables were chopped and prepared for cooking, Heimdall roasted an animal for us, which is another mortal Sunday ritual in this region of Midgard. I have complicated feelings about eating animals. I never did like the idea of mortals sacrificing animals in my name because, given how often I appear in animal form, they were risking sacrificing me to me!

(And sacrificing yourself to yourself is Odin's thing, I'm no copycat. Long story, involves a tree, some runes, and Odin dying, sort of.)

However, the roast flesh was delicious so I swallowed my guilt along with the crispy, crispy skin.

# Day Seven:
## Monday

In Topic the teacher said some words I did not listen to.

> Blah career blah skills blah your future blah money blah.

But, when I started listening again, I learned that we were discussing what we would do when we grow up. Valerie could not decide between jockey or paranormal investigator.

> I'm getting high ectoplasm readings here!

> Oh no! Not ghosts!

"I'll probably grow too big to be a jockey," said Valerie, with a shrug. "So I think I'll be a paranormal investigator. I've asked Georgina if she'd like to start a detective agency but she wants to be a musician or a programmer." She looked at me. "If you were mortal, what would your dream job be?"

"Dream job?" I said, with a scoff. "I do not dream of labour!"

"OK, but what would you do if you had to choose a human job?" she asked. "Mortals can't just laze around doing nothing like gods."

This was not true. I have seen many photographs of wealthy mortals who appear to do nothing but lie in the sun on large sailing vessels buying things.

Today I think I shall buy Belgium.

But Valerie pointed out that I was *not* rich as a mortal, so she insisted I pick a profession.

I thought about it for a while. "If I had to select an occupation to perform in return for gold, I would be a star of stage and screen."

THE MAGNIFICENT LOKI

In town for one night only, you lucky, lucky things!

Valerie looked sceptical and turned to Thor. "What job would *you* do? Footballer?"

Thor's eyes lit up. "No! That was my first thought when we started the lesson, but actually I want to be a tree surgeon," he said. "I was reading this" – he held up the worksheet that had descriptions of various jobs – "and it says that tree surgeons help to keep trees healthy. If I were not a god keeping Asgard safe from giants, I think it would be a noble calling to protect trees. For is not Yggdrasil, the world tree, at the source of all life?"

"That's lovely!" said Valerie.

I made a disgusted noise. Thor is so wholesome it makes me feel physically ill. But I do think, sometimes, life would be simpler to be him. Not a thought in his pretty head! How quiet it would be!

I'm so pretty and my head is so empty it makes me feel as light as air!

SKIP
SKIP

I, Loki, have far too many thoughts. Yes, they are always clever, but sometimes it is tiring to be this brilliant.

After school, Georgina and I had our first detention. Two adults were present as well as our teacher. The teacher said they were parents of some twins in Coat Girl's year who were helping out with the fair.

"I'm Kris and this is Elsa," said one of them, pointing at the other. "We're on the fair committee with your parents."

"Thanks, I don't care," I said.

After giving us a list of items to make, Kris and Elsa scurried away to the parent meeting like the irrelevant insects they were. Our teacher gave us a lot of art materials, including something called papier mâché.

**Papíer mâché:** a sticky mix of glue, paper and other substances. It is used for sculptures and, when used in schools, seems to have the primary purpose of making children as sticky as possible.

Georgina was deeply scornful when I said we did not have such a substance in Asgard.

Our teacher told us to use our imagination to create the decorations for the fair. Then she looked suspiciously at me.

But not TOO much imagination, Liam.

I don't know what havoc she thought I could wreak with only art supplies?

You could probably end the world with only art supplies if you put your mind to it.

!

I appreciate your faith.

> **! It's not faith. It's terror. BEHAVE, Loki!**

Thor had to stay at school with us, because Heimdall and Hyrrokkin were at their fair committee meeting in another part of the building. Apparently the other parents would get suspicious if they left Thor at home because he's "only a child". See! I was right about child labour yesterday!

As Georgina and I sat down, Thor said he was going to patrol the school for giants.

We haven't been attacked by Frost Giants for a while. They will surely attack soon.

It's always giant this, giant that with you.

After Thor left, I asked Georgina if she was still angry with me about the punishment.

"Why would I be angry with you?" she said. Her face was motionless, except for her lips.

I'm only in the worst trouble of my life. My dad only told me he didn't recognize me with this behaviour. My mum only did this thing with her mouth that I've only seen her do when she sees people spitting in the street. Oh, and I'm only not able to go riding until the punishment is over. I can't RIDE, Loki. I can't RIDE. But no, I'm not angry.

"Oh good!" I began.

"I'm not angry," she went on.

You're just dead to me.

But I don't want to be dead to you! I want us to be friends.

67

"That ship has sailed. It's in the distance now. It's probably going to fall off the edge of the world and get eaten by sea monsters," said Georgina.

GRRR

The Friend-ship

"Let's just get this punishment over and then I never have to speak to you again," she finished.

"But what about Valerie?" I said, offering an argument that I thought might work on Georgina, whose fondness for Valerie is comparable to Thor's fondness for hammers. "What if she wants us all to spend time together?"

I simply won't speak to you. I'll speak to Valerie only.

THREATENING SNIP

(( ))

I decided in that moment I was going to make Georgina love me!

I'll admit, that could have gone better.

I will try to get Georgina to like me *without* mind control.

Good luck with that... !

After detention, I asked Hyrrokkin and Heimdall how to get people to like you when they hate you.

"You must continue to work on becoming a better person," said Hyrrokkin. "I can't guarantee it will make people like you, but it's the right thing to do."

69

That all sounded very pointless. Why be good if I didn't get anything out of it?

"In my new parenting book, it says you should focus on showing empathy to others," Heimdall said.

ENSURE YOUR CHILD BECOMES A PROFITABLE MEMBER OF CAPITALIST SOCIETY BY SHOWING EMPATHY

"Empathy is when you try to put yourself in someone else's shoes," he explained.

I didn't see why stealing someone's shoes was a way to become a better person. If I tried it, I know it would lead to great wrath and many punishments.

Give me back my shoes, Liam!

# Day Eight:
## Tuesday

There was a new boy in class today. This aroused
great distrust in me. The last time we had a new pupil
in class, it turned out to be the goddess Sif in disguise,
Hel-bent on revenge. And revenge against *me*, which
is the worst kind of revenge. This boy even looked
vaguely familiar, with long hair, very pale skin and
large eyes.

But I couldn't quite place him.

The most worrying thing, however, was
not that he looked familiar to me. It was that
he was *already* familiar to everyone else.

Where do
I know you
from?

They were all acting as though he had *always* been in our class. This was highly suspect and I did not like it in the slightest.

In Handwriting, the teacher scolded the strange child for not paying attention. Then, under her breath, muttered, "Typical Alfie, always off with the fairies."

Alfie? How did she know his name? He had not said it! And how could anything he'd done today be "typical" since he only arrived this morning?

I did not like this situation one little bit.

AT BREAK

Hi, Alfie.

Hey, bud, want to play sportsball?

Chatting like old friends →

I had to get to the bottom of this sinister mystery.

At the end of school, I decided to follow "Alfie" and confront him. But I could not get him alone, for he and Valerie were walking together.

Surely they'll split up soon?

Yet when Valerie reached her home and her mums came to the door, they embraced *both* children, then all of them went inside together.

What? WHAT???

When I arrived home, Thor and I were ordered to take Fido for a walk. Hyrrokkin told me that I enjoy it really! Me? Enjoy being seen in public with a creature as servile as a tame DOG? Unlikely.

FIVE MINUTES LATER...

WHO'S A GOOD BOY? YOU'RE A GOOD BOY! I TOO AM A GOOD BOY AND SOMETIMES A GOOD GIRL BUT NO ONE SAYS IT TO ME! YOU'RE THE BEST DOG! Ahem. I mean you're OK.

As we walked, I probed Thor casually and subtly about Alfie. "Let's talk about Alfie," I began.

Thor just grunted, but I pressed. "In order to become a better mortal, Heimdall says I should try to put myself in the shoes of others. Please help me put myself in Alfie's shoes."

Thor looked a little touched at that.

73

"Alfie ... he's Valerie's cousin, remember? He lives with her. He's just ... one of the gang. Alfie. Everyone knows Alfie."

Was it my imagination, or did Thor's eyes look glassy? Could Alfie be using ... *magic*?

The idea of a mortal child with access to powerful magic was not a relaxing one. Or, not to sound like Thor, but could Alfie be a giant in disguise? At home, to distract myself from that horrifying thought, I decided to play a game on my phone. I was just about to defeat a particularly tricky digital enemy when...

## ⇛ RAP RAP! ⇚

I made a dignified and reasonable sound of alarm.

! **Lie detected. You squealed like a stuck pig.**

Well, what was I supposed to do? It was VERY surprising.

Anyway, I looked around me and there, tapping at my bedroom window, was Alfie. This was a surprise in many respects. Mostly because my bedroom is NOT ON THE GROUND FLOOR.

I grasped my wand. Then I opened the window.

"So," said Alfie. "I have returned!"

"This implies you have been here before. I don't know you. Unlike, apparently, everyone else."

"You do not recognize me?" said Alfie. Moonlight glinted off surprisingly sharp canines as a beautifully nasty smile spread across his face.

"I may not have seen you before," I said, "but I know I don't like you. You have an irritating face and your hair..." His long silky locks whipped around him in a faint breeze ... revealing his ears.

Only then did I realize at whom I was looking.

"It is I, Vinir! Here to rain vengeance upon the most pathetic of gods!" said Vinir, unnecessarily.

"Yes, yes, the ears gave it away," I said.

"Why are you here disguised as a mortal child?"
I asked.

"When last we met you taunted me to pick on someone my own size," said Vinir. "So I altered my size using complex wand magic. I did not merely rely upon an elven glamour but TRULY changed my size, casting a spell on the people around you to believe I had always been here, so I could go about my fateful business undisturbed!"

He puffed out his skinny chest with pride. The arrogant turd.

"You didn't get the ears right though, did you?"
I pointed out.

Natural talent

"I chose not. Mortal ears are so ugly," he snarled.

"Some of us can shape-shift NATURALLY," I said.

"Then you earn no glory for your effort," sniffed Vinir. "Enough talk! I am here for our magical duel. I shall now perform the ancient elvish contract song!"

Oh Loki of Asgard, worthless cur
We two will duel unto the death
The spell whose name is Perilous
An ancient spell that drains the life from each
Until the strongest wins
And then, the weakest slithers into death

It didn't even rhyme, although I do admit he had a beautiful voice. Sweat pricked my skin and I laughed nervously. "I have an alternative proposal to us duelling to the death."

"Oh?" said Vinir.

"We *don't*," I said. "And you go away."

Vinir's wide eyes flashed with rage and he raised his wand as though to kill me on the spot. "Impudent whelp! You lily-livered, craven villain! I ought to turn you inside out and throw your innards to the dogs!"

EW.

I had, on reflection, perhaps been a little too flippant. Even in child form, this elf clearly had control over powerful wand magic that is beyond even my considerable skills.

Plus, he seemed really, really cross.

But I, Loki, possess a mighty power that none can resist. My enemy was powerless in the face of my prowess!

**Did you use a spell?**　　　　　　　　　　　!

No, silly. My own innate magic.

**Oh, so did you turn into a bird and fly away?**　!

77

I mean my greatest magic.

My ability to talk my way out of anything.

! I'd say that's more an irritating personality trait than a power.

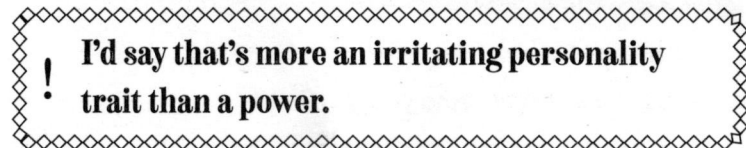

Do not take my name in vain!

You say potato, I say shut up.

"I can't duel with you on a school night," I stalled.

Vinir threw back his head and laughed. It sounded like tinkling bells. Evil tinkling bells.

Mwahahaha!

"I do not care about mortal school nights!" he said. "Mortals are little more than animals!"

But this reminded me of what he *did* care about...

Worked last time, shall we give it another whirl?

Sensitivity button

DADDY DEAREST

VINIR-O-TRON 2000

Giving him an innocent look, I said, "You are clearly FAR more advanced in your magical skills than I. You don't want to go home and tell your father you defeated an unworthy opponent in a duel, do you?"

Using someone's insecurities against them isn't original ... but it works every time.

Very well.

"I will give you time to prepare," he said, flipping his hair out of his eyes.

Honestly, has he not heard of hairbands? Or haircuts? Maybe I will slip into his room in the night and give him the Sif treatment.

"You have until the moon is at its fullest, the day after the mortals celebrate winter at their so-called fair," said Vinir, with a deep and sweeping bow.

That gave me a little under a month to think of a way out of this. Plenty of time for my genius mind!

"Very gracious of you," I said. "Until then, get back off home to Elfland or wherever you live."

Vinir shook his long pale finger. "I am not going

home. I will stay on the mortal plane, to make sure you don't run away like the coward you are."

DRAT. Running away was my number one plan!

"At least free my friends and my fake family from your glamour," I said.

"I told you it is NOT a glamour," growled Vinir. "It is a spell. Glamours are easy! A spell to bend reality like this takes real skill!"

"Well, whatever it is, can you free my friends from it, please?" I said.

Actually, the reason I wanted my friends freed was so they would discover that Alfie was an evil elf of murderous intent, and help me defeat him.

But, er, freeing them for their own sake was good too.

## Too little, too late.    !

"I shall now depart," said Vinir. "These mortal child bodies appear to need a lot of sleep. But from tomorrow I will dog your footsteps until I have my satisfaction in our duel! I will haunt you like the undead draugr who snap at the heels of men! Indeed, I will be as the dark shadow of the fates, those Norns who weave all our destinies! I shall be ever present to foreshadow your inevitable doom," he finished, with a flourish.

↑
Draugr

Basically, he was OBSESSED with me.

"Until then, farewell, bad god," he said.

And off he flew into the night, like a pale, annoying bat.

# Day Nine:

## Wednesday

After a night of very unsettling dreams, morning came. As Vinir promised, he undid the spell that had convinced my friends and fake family that he was a normal mortal child.

And then I got a text from Valerie.

I remember it all now. He's an ELF? I have an ELF living with me??? It's like Lord of the Rings in my sitting room! And aliens are actually elves! OMG!

I discussed the situation with Heimdall, Hyrrokkin and Thor over breakfast.

Heimdall, predictably, referred to one of his horrible parenting books.

This says you should encourage your children to face their fears head on.

HOW TO STOP YOUR KIDS FROM WHINING SO MUCH

"But my fear is a fear of being killed!" I pointed out. "Do you want me to die?"

"No," said Hyrrokkin. She put a hand on my arm.

83

But you are capable of so much more than you believe, Loki.

"How will I find out what I'm capable of if I'm dead?" I muttered. But her words did bring a certain kind of warmth to my heart. The warmth did not cancel out the terror, mind you.

Thor ssssucks!

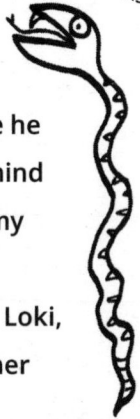

"Why don't you simply try to win the duel?" said Thor.

As if! Thor was used to winning every battle he fought. (With a few exceptions. Long story, remind me to tell you about the time when he fought my son – the great sea serpent, Jormungand – and failed to kill him. That's my slippery boy!) But I, Loki, was not accustomed to victory in battle. Whether magical or otherwise.

I'm a lover not a fighter.

A lover of running away from fights, that is.

84

I pointed out that Thor's idea would end in tears (mine) and death (also mine), but Hyrrokkin asked how I could possibly be sure I would not win this fight, given that I had run away from every previous conflict that presented itself.

How do you know you always lose if you never try?

Just my luck, being stuck with a fake parent who is very logical and uses it against me. Rude!

Hyrrokkin asked me about the spell that I had to use in the duel. When I told her the name of the spell, she went a little pale, but then swallowed and smiled.

"This is a difficult spell to master. But as long as you practise, you will be able to do it," she said.

"Difficult?" I said. The spell looked fairly simple in fact. Only one ingredient, barely any words.

Hyrrokkin explained that battle magic is simple in its obvious components – the words, the gestures, the ingredients – because all spells on a battlefield must be swift.

Hold on. I must harvest the tears of an elk and— ERK!

WHOOSH

My spell is speedy. Sucks to be you!

However, the gestures had to be incredibly precise, and the state of mind was vital, requiring a great deal of self-control.

Self-control? Oh no. I am doomed. I can control others, certainly, but as a god of chaos with a suitably chaotic inner life, controlling myself was another matter!

"You must practise until you can get into the right emotional state even in the most dangerous of circumstances. I will help you, but I cannot do it for you," Hyrrokkin explained. "You must repeat the spell so often – and so well – that the gestures become second nature, not a fraction out of place, and your emotions settle instantly into the correct arrangement for the spell to work."

Emotional self-control AND precision?

My friend, you are in deep doo doo.

I *had* to find a way out of this fight. I texted Valerie about it.

What should I do???

I'm not sure. Perhaps Hyrrokkin is right? You should just practise the spell.

Practise? Me? What kind of peasant do you take me for?

Everyone has to practise things! I have to practise my riding even though I've been doing it for years!

OK but can't you throw Vinir out of your house so he has to go home?

He didn't take the spell off my parents so no I can't. Anyway he'd only come back for the duel. Keeping him here means I can spy on him and look for weaknesses!

When I arrived in the playground, Valerie and Vinir were deep in conversation. Georgina was standing with them, looking a little put out. Valerie did NOT look like she was spying on Vinir. She looked fascinated!

Hi.

Hi, Loki.

"So, every time a human has thought they were abducted by aliens ... it was elves?" asked Valerie, scribbling down notes.

> Yes.

> Well, almost every time.

Valerie leaned forward eagerly, her pen poised mid-scratch. "So you're saying aliens could still be real?"

> I'm on the edge of my seat. ARE we real?

Vinir laughed. It sounded like nails down a chalkboard to my ears ... if those nails were really beautifully filed and instead of a chalkboard they were rippling over a harp. OK, I admit, he has a delightful laugh, OK? I still hate him.

"Aliens could very well be real," said Vinir. "We elves are not so self-centred as to believe everything is about us. Unlike gods."

POINTED LOOK ←

88

> Aliens! We could have elves AND aliens!

At that, Georgina let out an exasperated sigh. Could it be that she disliked Vinir? Perhaps this would bring us closer?

"This is all fascinating," I said, in a tone that made it clear that it was, in fact, so boring I was seconds away from a near-fatal coma. "But we have to get to lessons."

"I hate saying Liam's right but we do have to go," said Georgina.

"I'm right, you say?" I asked, linking arms with her. "I knew we would very soon be the best of friends once again!"

But Georgina shook me off. "I'm not talking to you except when I have to."

"You just said 'Liam's right!' to me," I objected.

The elbow of rejected friendship

"I said that ABOUT you," she said.

"But Vinir took the spell off you! That means we're friends! I asked him to take the spell off my friends!"

"No, it means YOU think we're friends," said Georgina, and left for her next lesson.

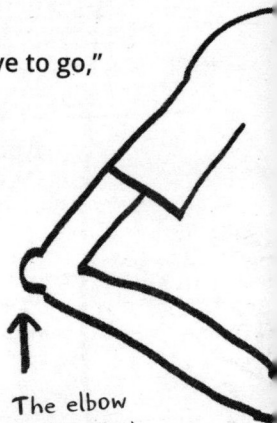

"I might still need your assistance in winning over Georgina," I said to Valerie.

But Valerie wasn't listening. She was too busy finishing off her notes.

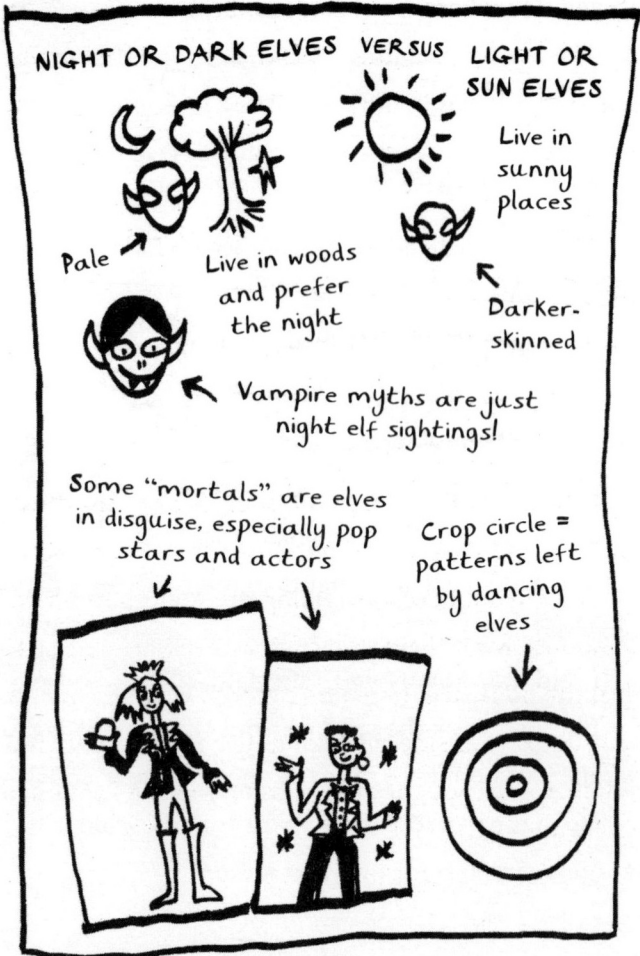

NIGHT OR DARK ELVES VERSUS LIGHT OR SUN ELVES

Live in sunny places

Pale →

Live in woods and prefer the night

Darker-skinned

Vampire myths are just night elf sightings!

Some "mortals" are elves in disguise, especially pop stars and actors

Crop circle = patterns left by dancing elves

In computing class, I created a simple computer program to generate excellent insults to use against your enemy. The teacher complimented my programming but queried whether the insults verged on bullying a specific student.

INSULT ALFIE

Alfie, you long-haired fiend.

Well, it WAS an enemy insult generator. So I was merely making the program accurate about my enemy! After all, hadn't she said...

Precision is very important in coding!

After school, I opened the spell book to try the spell Vinir said we would be using against each other.

The introduction describing the spell went on and on about how difficult the spell was to perform, so I shut the book in exhaustion before I even reached the spell itself. I considered asking Hyrrokkin to help me but even the thought of discussing the spell sounded tiring and dreary.

I needed another plan.

# Day Ten:
## Thursday

**LOKI VIRTUE SCORE OR LVS:**

# –650

Usually I'd dock points for insulting people, but Vinir/Alfie IS plotting your death, so on this occasion I will let it slide.

During detention with Georgina, I set about the epic task of getting her to see that I am an excellent person. I used a tactic Heimdall had told me about from his empathy book. It's called "listening". The idea is you – and I realize this is an outlandish idea for one as witty as I – cease speaking and, instead, remain silent while another speaks.

You are allowed to speak under *some* circumstances though.

Now what WERE the rules?

Asking the person questions about themselves ✔️

Asking them to repeat something you didn't quite hear or understand ✔️

Making encouraging noises such as "Mmm" or "Ooh" to imply they should continue their inane prattling ✔️

Changing the subject to yourself ❌

The most challenging part of the whole exercise is that, while they are speaking, you cannot simply wander off in your mind to more interesting topics. You must ABSORB what they are telling you.

As we set up our materials to start creating decorations, according to the list that the insignificant mortal parents had given us, I did not speak. But I had no opportunity to listen because Georgina did not speak to me. So, when we began our labours, I asked her questions.

"How was your day?" I asked, most virtuously, for I did not care what had happened at school. All days here are a monotonous parade of despair and pain.

"Why do you want to know?" Georgina asked, suspiciously.

LIE → I am merely interested in your experiences.

93

Georgina narrowed her eyes. Nevertheless, it appeared she was in the mood to speak, even if she didn't trust her conversation partner.

"I made a new program in Computing," she said. "It's a music program that plays musical scores out loud."

"That sounds..." I struggled to find a response that was not "absolutely worthless".

Luckily, she continued speaking.

"At break I played football with Isaac," she added, giving me a pointed look, as though expecting me to be both familiar with this child and, perhaps, guilty about something related to him. "My little brother."

"Ah, that sounds..." Again, I struggled with a response that would be suitable. I wished to say "incredibly tedious". But then I had a brainwave. "That sounds ... nice!"

For nice *is* merely a polite way of saying "incredibly tedious", so I didn't have to lie!

It was OK.

"What's wrong?" I asked, which is another of the things you are allowed to say when you are being a good listener.

# Day Eleven:
## Friday

**LOKI VIRTUE SCORE OR LVS:**

# -450

**200 points gained for listening to Georgina.
Keep it up! But, you know, faster and better.**

At the start of the day, our class teacher announced
that we would be starting a new project in Topic on
Monday and we needed to do some preparation.

When she announced that it was a group project,
I perked up. A group project means I can let others do
all the work! Especially with Valerie on my team!

Unfortunately the teacher chose Thor and Vinir to
be on my team as well. On the upside, spending more
time with Vinir could teach me his weaknesses...

> Knowing your enemy is the first step to defeating them.

At least I think that's something Odin said once.
Or I might have read it in one of Heimdall's many
self-help books. His new crop of books from the
library have been ... interesting.

HOW TO
LEAD LIKE
A CRIMINAL
MASTERMIND
Inspiration from
the greatest
bloodthirsty
crimes in
history!

How to Win
Friends and
Eviscerate
People:
Vlad the
Impaler's
Life Lessons

Who Moved
My Axe?
How to
change
when
change is
violent

The teacher told us all about our project. We had
to come up with an idea for a business and write a
business plan for a product or service that we could
sell at the school fair.

Did this mean we would *finally* be paid for all the
time we spent at school, as we should be? JOY! *And*
get paid to attend the fair? ELATION!

BOIING!

But there was no joy. All money raised would go to the school to pay for new books. BOOKS! I would spend the money on things FAR more imaginative than books!

We also had to choose roles to play in this imaginary business of ours. I, of course, would be the boss. I announced this to the group, expecting grateful acquiescence.

"You don't have any leadership qualities," pointed out Thor.

"I do!" I said. "The qualities needed in a boss are doing no work and making everyone do it for you, then taking the credit." I'd learned this definition from my trusty Guide to Mortal Life in the 21st Century after Heimdall's promotion.

**Boss:** in a system that mortals call Capitalism (see: Capitalism), this is the person who does the least actual work, yet gets paid the most while taking all the credit. The main tasks of a boss are tyranny and sitting in rooms talking about their weekend plans. These are called meetings.

We voted and, sadly, the others voted for Valerie to be the boss, even though she clearly planned to actually do her work and therefore would not be a proper boss.

Democracy is displeasing!

In Music, Ms Loach asked us to come up with jingles for our imaginary businesses. For a jingle, we needed a name, so Vinir and I argued about what the company should be called. I wanted it to have a name that was rude in a way the teachers wouldn't notice. Vinir wanted to name the company after his father.

"You would," I sneered. "Do you have a topic of conversation that does NOT involve your father?"

"I have many," said Vinir, frowning with his elegantly arched eyebrows. "But why should I waste good conversation on someone who only has a little while to live?" Then he threw back his head and laughed his irritating, tinkling laugh once again.

Right. I was going to fight this duel. And I was going to win. That would stop him tinkling all over the place.

Oh no, I have wet myself with fear. I need new elf pants.

Well, tinkling with *laughter* anyway.

At lunchtime, Thor was looking gloomy. I decided this was an excellent moment to demonstrate my listening skills again.

"What's wrong?" I asked.

"What do you want?" asked Thor, instantly suspicious.

"I merely wish to know what ails my dear fake brother," I said.

"If you really want to know, I was watching you and Vinir insulting each other in class and thinking how you used to insult ME," grumbled Thor. "Now you've got a new enemy and forgotten all about me."

"I will always have time and energy to insult you, Captain Fart Hammer," I said affectionately. "You look like a potato with hair."

Thor reacted by farting on me.

ARRGH!

GOD OF BUMTHUNDER STRIKES AGAIN!

# Day Twelve:
## Saturday

Heimdall, who seems to fancy himself as the god of wholesome weekend activities, decided that we should try a new board game as a family. The one he selected was a game in which you have to conquer every country in the world like a terrifying dictator.

Hmm.

CONQUER ALL!
Fascist fun for all the family!

OOH!

WOOF!

It'd be more fun with real battles.

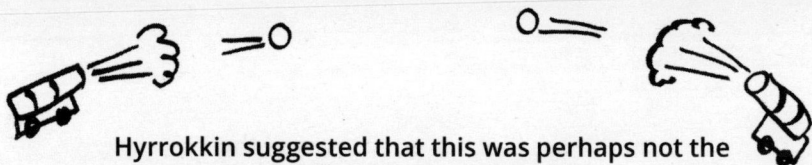

Hyrrokkin suggested that this was perhaps not the best idea, given that I did recently try to take over the world in real life.

"That's why it's perfect," said Heimdall. "This game provides a safe outlet for Loki's megalomaniac tendencies in a controlled situation!"

Suddenly the game sounded MUCH more interesting.

Sadly, I lost every round. I soon decided that it was a pointless game and, anyway, we couldn't play any more because the board had mysteriously fallen into the bin when everyone stopped to make a cup of tea.

After Heimdall made me clean and dry the board, I went to the park with Valerie and Fido. Annoyingly Thor came too, since my behaviour during the game meant I couldn't be trusted to roam freely that day. Georgina was there too, which presented me with the perfect chance to charm her.

FOUL STENCH

Even though I let her go first on all the slides, swings, roundabouts and other juvenile entertainments, Georgina did not speak to me other than to say a cold "thank you" each time.

When she and Thor started kicking a ball around, I swung on the swings next to Valerie.

Will Georgina ever be my friend again? I am trying my hardest.

You could just be normal with her and not try so hard?

Ridiculous! Only tedious people are normal.

"I think you have bigger problems," Valerie went on, wrinkling her forehead. "Vinir spent all this morning practising the spell for the duel. He got up at 4 a.m. to begin and he was still at it when I left to come here. I'm worried, Loki."

"Pshaw!" I said, waving her concern away. "I'm sure I will think of something."

"You have less than two weeks," said Valerie.

Which put me RIGHT off my swinging.

# Day Thirteen:
## Sunday

Hyrrokkin set me some exercises to help me get into the right state of mind for my spell. I had to sit very still and chant some ancient giantish words. I suppose mortals would call it meditation. I call it boring.

I'm being still.
I'm being still.
Can I stop yet?

I practised for a whole twenty minutes. I think that's a practising record for me!

But then a howl of rage summoned me downstairs to see what was happening. I needn't have hurried. It was merely Hyrrokkin, angered by a message on her phone.

"How dare they!" she growled, showing the phone to Heimdall as I peered over his shoulder.

Look at this! What monsters!

**WINTER FAIR GROUP CHAT**

PARENT ELSA:

I thought it would be nice if we all went for a drink to get to know each other better.

So far, that did not seem obnoxious. Hyrrokkin is moderately social and likes ale.

"Read on," she said, scrolling down.

**WINTER FAIR GROUP CHAT**

OVERLY ENTHUSIASTIC FATHER WHO RUNS THE BOOKSHOP:

Even better! Why don't we turn the drink into a brainstorming session. I know we have a lot of plans already for the fair, but we could be even more ambitious! Let's make this an occasion to remember!

MOTHER OF THE COATED ONE:

Great idea! I could definitely take on some more things. @Hyrrokkin, I don't believe you've committed to anything except pre-tearing the tickets for the raffle. Perhaps we could all help come up with something extra for you to do?

OVERLY ENTHUSIASTIC FATHER WHO RUNS THE BOOKSHOP:

Marvellous! I'll send deets for somewhere to meet, 8 p.m. tonight? Gorgeous! See you all then!

I want to rend them all limb from limb. Why must they take the emptiness of their own lives and make it MY problem?

*Welcome to MY life*, I thought, but decided it was not a good time to say this out loud.

"Hyrrokkin, if it pains you so much, I could handle this alone," said Heimdall, putting a hand on her arm. "My participation is enough cover for us to appear as normal mortals."

Hyrrokkin sighed deeply. "No, I will remain involved. I too must experience the fullness of mortal life. And forcing yourself to do things that make you miserable in order to appear normal, while complaining loudly to your spouse about it, appears to be a key part of their existence."

# Day Fourteen:
## Monday

In Topic, we started our project in earnest. Our first task was to decide what product or service we would sell at the fair.

Vinir suggested we make jewellery. "My father is the greatest elven smith in history, and he has taught me much of his craft."

"Didn't he murder people and make jewellery out of their skulls?" asked Valerie. "I read it in a myth."

"Yes, but it was sublimely beautiful jewellery," said Vinir, with a haughty sniff.

"I don't think we should sell things made with body parts at the school fair, even if they're pretty," said Valerie, grimacing.

The discussion continued. It was an excellent chance for me to observe Vinir and probe him for weakness.

"Let's think about this creatively," I suggested. "We should all imagine that WE are the product ... and say what's good about us ... and, more importantly, what's weak, bad or otherwise vulnerable about ourselves."

> I don't understand.

"So, Vinir," I said, ignoring Thor. "You go first. Why don't we start with your weaknesses? The chinks in your armour? The ways in which you are ... easy to destroy?"

> How is this going to help us come up with a product?

> Shh! Don't be rude! Let Vinir speak.

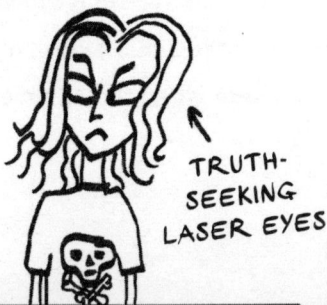

TRUTH-SEEKING LASER EYES

"Nice try, Loki," Vinir said. "I'm not going to tell you my weaknesses."

RATS!

"OK, we really do need to think of a product to sell at the fair," said Valerie, as the teacher glanced over to our table, eyes full of suspicion. "Or..." Valerie looked at the worksheet. "We could choose a service? We could wash people's cars if they're driving to the school fair? I've seen a lot of children dropped off in VERY dirty cars."

CLEAN ME...

Honk if u luv squalour

POOH3AD

SERIOUSLY. I AM BEGGING YOU. I AM FOUL.

Because I am lazy, Thor is unimaginative, and Vinir is an immortal elf who has no particular attachment to doing well during his brief time at school, we all went with Valerie's idea.

111

After school, it was detention again. Having tired of snowflakes, I moved on to animals.

Aren't you a beauty?

ONE I MADE EARLIER

"You can't have polar bears and penguins in the same place," said Georgina, as she painted the door to her ice palace. "They're from different poles. Literally opposite ends of the globe."

"But they will both look adorable together," I said, which was all the justification I required.

"Fine, ignore reality like you always do," said Georgina.

"Also, they're on the list," I said, tapping the list we'd been given from the winter fair committee.

Georgina had no answer to that.

Steam of seeing my excellent points

Loki is clearly correct.

What she's probably thinking

# Day Fifteen:
## Tuesday

---

### LOKI VIRTUE SCORE OR LVS:

# -350

### Minus 25 points for academic laziness.

---

Even though there was no detention after school, Thor and I were forced to stay late because Heimdall and Hyrrokkin had a winter fair meeting. What wanton cruelty!

Or so I thought until I realized that being at school unsupervised after hours had its advantages. As Thor stalked the school looking for giants, I located the teachers' shower room. For an enjoyable hour or so, I found a way to hide a beef stock cube in the shower head. Next time a teacher showers there after cycling into work, they will smell of meaty soup.

BEEF?

After a while, Thor came to tell me that he'd found a frozen pipe.

BRR

"It must be Frost Giants!" he said.

"Or, and perhaps we should consider this option first, it might just be a frozen pipe," I suggested. "It IS winter." I gestured to Thor's thick coat. "Heimdall had to buy you a winter coat the other day!"

Thor was not convinced.

When Heimdall and Hyrrokkin's meeting ended, they came to fetch us, bringing with them some mortal adults whom I recognized.

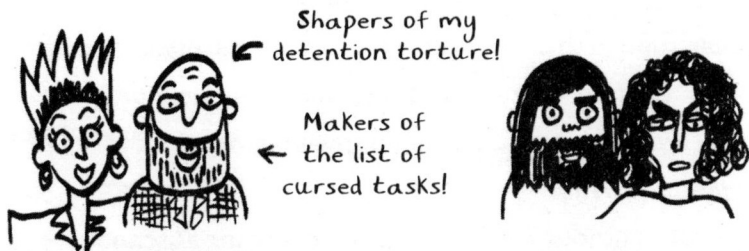

Shapers of my detention torture!

Makers of the list of cursed tasks!

Given Hyrrokkin's reactions to the winter fair chat group, I wondered whether she had brought them here to murder them.

Oddly, she looked delighted by their company. "Liam, Thomas, meet our new friends, Elsa and Kris."

We've met.

Hi!

I gave Hyrrokkin an irritable look. "I thought you hated everything about your ridiculous organizing committee?" I went on, gesturing to Kris and Elsa.

That's the thing. They hate it as much as we do!

We bonded over our mutual loathing of volunteering.

It's not volunteering. We were bullied into it. We hate every person on that committee.

"See?" Hyrrokkin grinned. "They're a delight."

"Here's to being slackers together," said Elsa, giving Hyrrokkin a high five.

As a mortal child, it is my duty to visibly find my parents embarrassing in public, so I made sure I kept up our cover story by fake vomiting at this public display of exuberance by someone so old.

"He's EXACTLY how you described him," said Elsa, chuckling.

"That's my son," said Hyrrokkin, tousling my hair.

This was essentially an act of war. My hair is sacred! But only a fool would meet Hyrrokkin in battle, so I contented myself with a very sarcastic smile. Hopefully her soul was wounded if not her body.

When we got home, Heimdall and Hyrrokkin were talking excitedly about their new friends.

"I'm so glad we met them," said Heimdall.

"Yes, at least SOME good has come out of our hideous labours," Hyrrokkin agreed.

"You do realize you've made friends with the people who came UP with the theme for the fair and were responsible for the form my torture sessions take?" I pointed out.

"Well," said Hyrrokkin, "everybody makes mistakes. And since they have clearly grown to hate their involvement with the committee, that's all right by me. Now, shall I help you practise your spell?"

I did not want to practise my spell. I wanted Kris and Elsa to atone for their role in my punishment.

Instead I contented myself with half an hour of unsuccessful spell practice as supervised by Hyrrokkin, followed by playing some ultra-violent computer games to chase the feelings of failure and dread from my soul.

Player: Tricksta
Health:
Lives:

My new game character

# Day Sixteen:
## Wednesday

**LOKI VIRTUE SCORE OR LVS:**

# -500

Minus 150 points for beef shower. You're going in the wrong direction! Reverse!

After school, Heimdall said he had some good news. In hopes of a pony, or perhaps at least a takeaway, I felt excitement rise in my heart ...

... only to have it dashed when the "good news" was merely that he had a new role in the winter fair.

"I will be playing Santa Claus!" Heimdall put his hand to his chest, clearly touched.

This is a role of great honour in such mortal celebrations!

**Santa Claus:** mystical being who brings presents for children and is connected to the concept of Christmas, a holiday in the religion that replaced the worship of the Norse gods in the northern regions. Odin has banned mention of Christmas in Asgard because it always puts him in a bad mood.

In conclusion: BAH HUMBUG.

Personally, as I am not a vain or self-centred god, I was not upset when Christianity replaced the worship of the Aesir.

Correction: you ARE a vain and self-centred god. You were merely not upset when Christianity replaced the Aesir because hardly anyone worshipped you in the first place and you found delight in seeing Thor and Odin's mortal popularity decline.

!

OK, I will admit, that was rather delicious.

After dinner, Hyrrokkin helped me practise my spell in the living room. My mind kept wandering and Hyrrokkin got increasingly annoyed with me.

I felt a hot ball in my throat that was half sob, half fury.

"It's not like I WANT to lose! I want to win VERY MUCH INDEED given that losing this battle means having all the life force sucked out of me!"

Hyrrokkin grabbed me by my puny mortal shoulders.

THAT'S WHY I'M BEING HARD ON YOU! Little Loki, I need you to win because I can't bear for you to die!

Hyrrokkin made me a cup of hot chocolate after that, with marshmallows. When I felt slightly less shaky, I asked a question that had been in the back of my mind for a little while.

"What *would* happen to me? If I died in this mortal body?" I asked, sipping the delicious hot chocolate.

Would I go to Hel?

Wander Midgard as a ghost?

Or to Valhalla? (Eternal feasts? Yay!)

Cease to exist?

Hyrrokkin shook her head. "Odin will not reveal to any of us what would happen if we were to die here. Part of living as a mortal is not knowing what happens after you die."

Typical Odin. He always has to be the one who knows everything, leaving the rest of us in the dark.

Hey!                                                    !

Do you detect a lie? Are you going to tell me Odin does not hoard knowledge like a dragon hoards treasure?

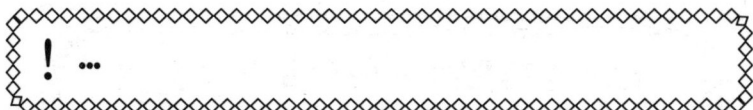

! ...

Thought so.

When I'd finished my hot chocolate, Hyrrokkin asked if I was ready to try the spell again. I shook my head and she gave me a little smile.

"Tomorrow," she said.

Perhaps my dreams shall reveal a way out of my deadly situation?

# Day Seventeen:
## Thursday

I did not dream of a solution. I dreamed of this instead.

Giant magic wand

Loki Kebab (Lokibab)

In Spelling, I watched Vinir closely, hoping to discover some weakness. But the only weakness he appeared to possess was poor spelling.

KARR WOSH

123

From her quizzing of Vinir, Valerie explained that elves don't use written language in Alfheim and they see correct spelling as irrelevant. It's not that they *cannot* spell, they simply consider spelling to be beneath them: written language is a matter of crude, unsubtle scrawlings, while living, spoken language is a joy.

I mean, we can agree on that. Hearing me speak IS delightful.

During detention, Georgina appeared stressed that we weren't going to be ready in time. Kris and Elsa had specified a certain number of animals and other decorations as part of their brief, and the teacher said that if we didn't make all of them, she would know we'd been slacking.

My parents are already so angry. If I fail detention, I don't want to know what they'll say.

Apparently Georgina, like Vinir, cares an immense amount about what her parents think. Not knowing my parents, I do not care at all what they think.

However, on seeing Georgina's worried expression, I redoubled my efforts to create wonderful decorations for this ridiculous winter fair. Not because I cared about doing a good job – I am FAR too glamorous and mysterious to worry about THAT – but because *Georgina* cared.

> **Careful, Loki! You're coming dangerously close to showing genuine empathy and performing a selfless act for someone else.** !

Do I get points for that?

> **Never mind. You're not THAT close.** !

# Day Eighteen:
## Friday

## LOKI VIRTUE SCORE OR LVS:

# -495

**A grudging 5 points for showing glimmers of empathy.**

School was the usual round of horror and pain. With added PE.

In the evening, Heimdall announced he was performing a mortal ritual known as the dinner party. Heimdall had carefully researched this ritual, and proudly declared it was vital for mortals of our intermediate level of wealth to invite other adults to our home in order to judge our cooking and interior décor.

Now remember, avoid any topics that might be controversial or cause arguments.

"That means politics is out, as is – based on my internet research, which led to strangers calling me names I shall not repeat – any mention of *Doctor Who*."

The guests would be Hyrrokkin and Heimdall's new friends Elsa and Kris from the winter fair committee. Before they arrived, Heimdall rushed around cleaning everything, even though there was no visible dirt anywhere. He had also, it transpired, spent all day cooking.

Once he'd stopped crying, Heimdall prepared me and Thor a sandwich before the mortal guests arrived. I thought perhaps this might mean we would be spared an evening of tedium with adults but, tragically, that was not the case.

"I want to make sure you aren't so hungry that you shame us in front of our friends by eating like pigs at the trough."

HOW DARE YOU!

Once I had washed the peanut butter from my face and hands and also my hair, the guests arrived. Fido bounded up to greet them eagerly.

He's fine, he doesn't bite.

No, but he does lick A LOT.

LICK
LICK
LICK

**At the party, the adults talked about:**

1. **Their jobs** (tedious)

Briefcase of boring

2. **The winter fair** (actually quite entertaining to see how angry they all were about it — also it transpired that Valerie's parents had refused to join the committee or even go to the school fair because they had better things to do, and all the adults agreed that they had to immediately become best friends with Valerie's mums as a result)

3. **The weather** (**WHY?**)

4. (Honestly, I stopped listening for a while and watched a spider building a web in the corner of the room. Pretty!)

5. **The cost of babysitters** (Kris and Elsa claimed to be paying a king's ransom to attend tonight)

**When they got on to point five I exclaimed, loudly:**

KILL ME NOW. PLEASE! DEATH WOULD BE A SWEET RELEASE!

← Embarrassed

← VERY embarrassed

129

Heimdall apologized profusely then sent me upstairs. If I'd known I could have escaped so easily I would have spoken up sooner!

When the guests left, Thor came upstairs.

"I have disturbing news," he said, sitting next to me on my bed. "I found ice in the kitchen."

"Oh?" I said, wondering where this was going, but not wondering very hard, given Thor's one-track mind.

"I think" – he lowered his voice – "those mortals are Frost Giants in disguise."

"Let me ask you a question," I said, leaning back on my bed and stretching out my legs. "Did you, by any chance, find the ice in ... the freezer?"

Thor wouldn't meet my gaze. "Maybe."

I raised an eyebrow.

Thor screwed up his face. "Well, OK, fine, if Kris and Elsa are ordinary mortals then we need to watch for Frost Giants in the near future. It has been too long since they attacked."

He *did* have a point there. Of course, I did not say this out loud. It does not do to encourage Thor in his Frost Giant obsession.

Instead, I asked whether I had missed anything else interesting.

Thor shook his head and flopped back on the bed. "I wanted to die of boredom."

"You should've done what I did," I said, as I lay beside him.

I was going to complain that I was the good one now. Well, one of the good ones. But then I remembered the time I nearly killed him during the school play, and we just lay there for a bit before Thor yawned and said he was going to bed.

As appears to be a new and unwelcome part of my bedtime hygiene rituals, I thought about the duel while brushing my teeth.

I heard my conscience, just then.

> You should do something about the duel. I worry that you are in denial about it.

"I am NOT in denial," I replied. Though, with a mouthful of toothbrush, it sounded more like:

MF 'OT IN ENIAL

Then, as I finished brushing my teeth, my conscience spoke again.

> You didn't floss.

> Sometimes being good is so NOISY inside your head.

! Yes, but I notice you STILL haven't flossed.

# Day Nineteen:
## Saturday

---

**LOKI VIRTUE SCORE OR LVS:**

# -600

**Minus 75 for disrupting the dinner party and -30 for not flossing. Not good enough!**

---

This morning, Valerie asked me to something called an escape room, which involves being locked in a room and trying to get out, for enjoyment.

I'm locking you in now.

YAY!

Imprisonment!

As someone who has been in prison, I did not see the appeal. But Valerie said that Vinir was coming, which meant I could observe him. Suitably, the theme of the escape room was Spy Mission – we were supposed to be spies who had to find all the secret codes in order to exit the room.

Unfortunately, we did not get to wear disguises and actually spy on people. It was, instead, a matter of doing mathematics for fun (allegedly).

Since Vinir is not interested in written symbols, and I do mathematics only under threat of detention, Valerie and Georgina solved most of the puzzles while we watched. This gave me time to question my enemy.

Spy in disguise

Gadget watch

Rocket boots

Given that Elves turn their irritatingly perfect noses up at the written word, how DO you learn magic?

From our elders, of course. From a young age every elf must repeat all the spells until they know them inside out.

Casual, cool, natural

134

"So, you've been doing magic for how long?"
A growing sense of despair began to flood through
my veins.

"Since my 100th birthday. So, around four
thousand years or so," he said airily. "By elven
standards, I am a mere beginner."

As someone who had been performing wand
magic for about a month, my emotional reaction
was roughly:

"Er, given your inclination towards honourable
conduct, do you think perhaps we should call off our
duel? You have a head start on me longer than some
human civilizations."

Vinir's mouth formed a grim line. "I sent word to
my father that I am duelling with you. I cannot back
down now. We must proceed."

TURDS. Perhaps he had some non-magical
weakness I could exploit.

Maybe I could do something with that? Shape-shift into his father mid-duel to distract him? The trouble was I didn't know what Daddy Dearest looked like.

"Do tell me more about your father. Especially the specifics of his physical form. Perhaps draw me a picture?"

136

"I know of your shape-shifting abilities, trickster. As we have established based on the multi-millennial timeline of my magical career, I was not born yesterday."

TURDS. Why can't all my foes be as easy to fool as Frost Giants? I was starting to miss those icy trollwits!

My conversation with Vinir was interrupted by Valerie and Georgina, who had solved the puzzle in "record time" according to the teenager at the front desk.

"We are the champions!" crowed Georgina.

"Victorious!" said Valerie.

"Impressive," said Vinir. "For mortals."

"I've been wondering something," Georgina went on. She had a certain glint in her eye. "You're an elf, right? So is that like Santa's elves?"

Vinir's nostrils flared with fury and it was a few moments before he could control himself enough to speak.

We. Are. Not. Like. Santa's. Elves. Never mention the name Santa around me again!

VENGEANCE ACHIEVED.

"Santa," I said quickly, with a wink towards Georgina.

She didn't wink back, but she *did* smirk.

RESULT!

"If I wasn't already going to kill you, I would wreak such terrible vengeance upon you, churl!" snarled Vinir.

"What have you got against Santa's elves?" said Georgina. "They're cute."

"I AM NOT CUTE! I am powerful and noble and honourable."

STOMP

STOMP

138

(OK, I admit, he was not actually dressed like that.)

"Elves DO make things though, like Santa's elves," said Valerie earnestly. My dear friend always *is* a stickler for accuracy. "Your father is a smith and makes jewels – like Santa's elves make toys – and he makes flying machines – like Santa's sleigh—"

"Yes, but he does NOT make gifts for small children," growled Vinir. Then, thinking about it, he added, "I suppose he did make those gifts *out* of small children."

"Have you ever considered that your father might not be a very good person?" I asked.

Vinir narrowed his eyes. "Have you ever considered that you are a weak, pathetic whelp who shall be dead at my hand before long?"

So, I suppose I should probably start practising my spell?

You really, really should. !

# Day Twenty:
## Sunday

Hyrrokkin has set me some exercises to help me practise my spell – today's were to repeat the gestures of the spell while attempting to clear my mind.

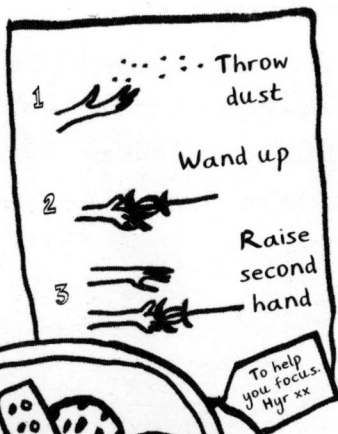

1 Throw dust

2 Wand up

3 Raise second hand

To help you focus. Hyr xx

Every time I attempted them, something distracted me. A message from Valerie. Hunger. Thirst. An interesting bird outside... What kind of bird was it? I decided to look it up online...

Hyrrokkin came in to find me blasting zombies in the head while sitting on the spell book. I do not know why; maybe I hoped knowledge would seep into my body via osmosis. Buttmosis rather.

"That does *not* look like practising your spell," she said. "Come on. You need to practise in order to win the duel." A look of worry passed across her face. "Please?"

"It's too hard," I said.

"We can do it together." Hyrrokkin held out her hand for the spell book. "Let us attempt the full spell. Perhaps seeing the parts in context will help you."

I got up and gave it to her, and she flipped to the right page.

141

STEP ONE: Throw a handful of dust into the air.

STEP TWO: Hold your wand with one hand and extend your other arm towards your enemy. Keep both arms steady.

STEP THREE: Repeat these words while sending your will out towards your enemy.

"To death. To dust. For ever."

I can't I can't I can't...

Let us try the whole thing. It might help you to focus on the practical side of the spell rather than over-thinking the mental part.

I nodded. I felt oddly nervous, even though this was just a practice.

Hyrrokkin pulled out an orange. "We're going to use an object that has traces of life force to practise on, pretending that it's Vinir. Picture draining his life force slowly at first, then faster and faster until he's empty. I'll show you. Though I will pretend it is my eternal nemesis, the head of the winter fair committee."

Hyrrokkin brushed the remains of the dead orange into the bin.

"Your turn." She placed another on the table. "Clear your mind, then focus on sucking the life force from the orange. Imagine that it is Vinir. Then throw the dust, perform the gestures, and say the words."

I picked up my wand. I considered taking some of the orange dust to use for the spell but the thought repulsed me, so I took some dust from the top of the computer.

**1.** I threw it in the air.

**2.** I extended my wand hand and held out my other arm beside it.

**3.** It was harder than it looked to keep both my puny arms still, but I managed it.

**4.** I focused on Vinir's irritatingly perfect face and swooshy hair. I said the words.

Nothing happened. I imagined the life force draining from the Vinir-Orange. I pictured Vinir fading into nothing.

I shook my wand. "Could this thing be broken?" I asked, tapping it on the wall in case that could knock

Plump and unwithered

some life into it. One thing I have learned in the mortal world is that many devices work again if you hit them. Sadly the same does not seem true of wands.

Hyrrokkin shook her head. "Your wand is fine. As were your gestures – and the words were spot on."

I felt a small glow of pride.

I fear you do not truly want Vinir dead.

The glow faded, replaced with irritation. How did Hyrrokkin know what I was thinking? She is not a seer who has visions of the inner worlds of gods and men! (Even if she does have an uncanny ability to tell when I'm lying about tidying my room.)

"Of course I want him dead! He's trying to kill me!" I complained.

Hyrrokkin played with her wand, tapping it against the palm of her hand, looking at me as though she was searching for something.

"Do you want to *kill* Vinir? Really?" she asked. She put away her wand and folded her arms. "Are you a killer, little Loki?"

"I tried to kill Thor recently, didn't I?" I pointed out, feeling a flash of horror as I remembered.

"But in the end you did not. Have you ever killed a person on purpose?" asked Hyrrokkin.

I shook my head.

She walked closer to me and put a hand on my shoulder. She smiled. "For the moment, let's forget about Vinir and use something I *know* you will want to destroy."

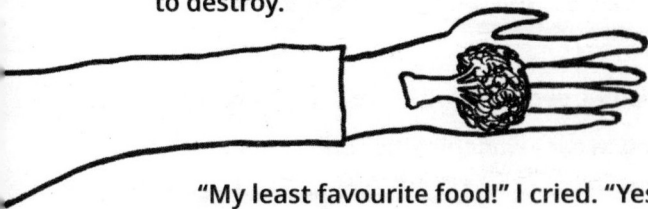

"My least favourite food!" I cried. "Yes, THIS I can destroy utterly!"

And, with a song in my heart, I nodded and pulled myself upright to perform the spell. I threw some of the dust at the broccoli, then held my wand out straight.

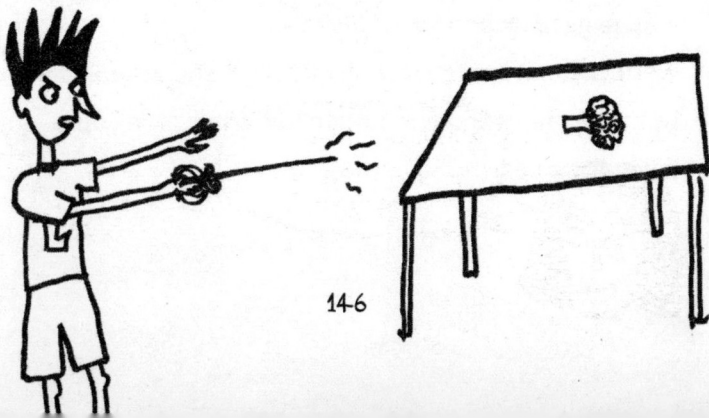

14-6

Focusing on my violent hatred of broccoli and my desire for it to cease its foul existence, I muttered the words. Power swelled inside me.

"Good, good, go on," muttered Hyrrokkin.

I kept my arms steady and continued repeating the words. I visualized drawing out what once had made the evil vegetable living and growing. I felt its life pass into me, and as my power grew, the broccoli began to shrivel. I could see it turning to dust in my mind. The broccoli grew drier and browner and sadder-looking but then...

You're going to die. You're going to die. You're going to die.

As the phrase repeated in my mind, the power subsided within me and all the life force returned to the broccoli. It was good as new.

I sagged. "I don't know what went wrong."

What went through your mind as the spell failed?

HAHAHA SUCKS TO BE YOU.

"I suddenly knew I was going to die when the duel happens. And I felt..." I touched my chest. *"Afraid."*

Hyrrokkin put a hand on my shoulder. "Clear your mind. Remember the exercises I gave you."

How could I forget them? Who knew boredom and horror could be so neatly combined in a single activity?

"Be in the spell. Focus on the spell only," Hyrrokkin went on.

Immediately, my mind was abuzz with a million thoughts.

You're going to die.

If you win you'll be a murderer. You're bad.

You're going to die.

You're going to die.

I wonder what's for dinner?

After two more hours of unsuccessful attempts, my hands trembling and my mind wandering ever further, Hyrrokkin suggested we take a break and go to the cinema.

It was surprisingly effective.

# Day Twenty-One:
## Monday

Tragic as this may sound, I was genuinely happy to go to school today. For, although school is torture, it at least distracted me from staring into the terrible face of death.

Unfortunately, every lesson found a way to remind me of what was ahead.

I'm not terrible, I'm just a little guy!

In Maths, I found myself counting the days until the duel that would end me. In Art, I found myself drawing an upsetting picture.

150

In Spelling, Vinir's spelling was so wildly off-mark that the teacher asked me to help him, so I was forced to aid my enemy.

I did take the enjoyable opportunity to patronize him. As I pointed out every single one of his spelling errors, he hissed, "Mortal spelling is beneath me. I refuse to trap beautiful language in this banal prison of letters!"

"You're just sore that there's something I can do better than you."

He fixed his furious eyes upon me and whispered, in the most even, calm tone, "I look forward to *ending* you, trickster."

I pulled myself up in my seat with great dignity. "Ordinarily, when someone comes to your aid in your hour of need, the correct response is 'thank you'. Clearly your father was too busy being a celebrity smith-slash-murderer to bother teaching you any manners."

He felt that. GOOD. If I couldn't defeat him in the duel, I could at least make him suffer first.

> ! This needless cruelty will be reflected in tomorrow's point score.

If I'm going to die anyway, why not have a little fun on the way down?

> ! I am so very, very tired.

I pushed Vinir further. "I bet your father is so disappointed. Look at you. What have you done with your many thousands of years? I've never heard of your deeds."

"I have done many ... deeds!" he said, faltering at the end.

Name one!

"I don't need to justify myself to you," sniffed Vinir, and turned away from me, leaning down over his work as though he was paying it the closest attention. He was biting his lip. The universal sign that a humanoid being is trying not to cry.

Once I was home after detention that evening, I was wandering towards the kitchen for a snack when I heard raised voices. Hyrrokkin and Heimdall were speaking loudly and angrily. Almost shouting.

"I cannot BELIEVE it was you who volunteered us for the fair!" Hyrrokkin growled. "Traitor. Monstrous traitor."

153

"I would rather die alone and friendless in a boiling desert than do what I must for this fair."

Hyrrokkin was in full furious flow.

I have to **BAKE CAKES!** Gluten-free, vegan **CAKES** with vanilla frosting spelling out **WINTER FAIR**. I, who defeated many foes on the field of battle. I, who tamed wild beasts and struck fear into the hearts of my enemies! I, who rode dragons over the nameless mountains of Jotunheim while the diamond-sharp ice storms raged!

While listening to them argue was amusing, what Hyrrokkin said at the end of the argument turned my glee to dread.

"We shouldn't be indulging in this mortal nonsense while Loki is in danger," said Hyrrokkin. "Given his lack of progress with the spell so far, he has no chance in this duel and we do not know what will happen if he dies on Earth."

GULP

154

Dread

Vom

Existential horror

Terror

"No, we don't," said Heimdall. "But you've been saying the whole time we've been here that Loki needs to learn lessons for himself. Can he not find triumph on his own?"

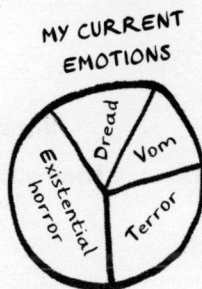

"There is no triumph in death," said Hyrrokkin.

I did a little sick in my mouth at that.

Hyrrokkin carried on, oblivious. "We've watched over him these past few months, protecting him – admittedly, mostly from himself – we cannot let him fall now."

Heimdall sighed. "Yes. You're right, you're right. All I want is to do the right thing for him. Ridiculous and infuriating as Loki is, I truly care for him. (And sometimes her.)"

I will confess, there was a certain warmth in my belly. Care? For Loki? I wasn't sure if I'd ever heard such delightful words before.

Heimdall sounded very serious as he said, "What should we do? Call Odin?"

"I think the time has come," said Hyrrokkin.

My insides churned at the thought. Odin would know that I had failed. That I needed rescuing.

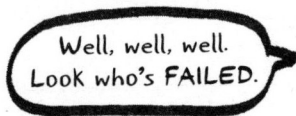

Well, well, well. Look who's **FAILED.**

155

But then again, I DID need rescuing. So maybe that would be OK?

Hey, Odin.

Moments later, there was a rap at the window.

## THIS IS AN OUT-OF-ASGARD RESPONSE

Odin is currently seeking prophecies concerning Ragnarok, the end of all things. He will manifest in your presence on his return, provided Ragnarok does not arrive while he is away. Sent on behalf of ODIN: Allfather of the gods of Asgard, Wisest of the Wise.

"Odin even told everyone he was off seeking prophecies and yet I KEEP having to deliver these messages," said Ratatosk the messenger squirrel, clicking her teeth. Then she scurried away into the night.

Heimdall shrugged. "Well, I suppose that just leaves us."

"I will redouble my efforts to aid him in his practice of the spell," said Hyrrokkin, nodding as though to convince herself this would work.

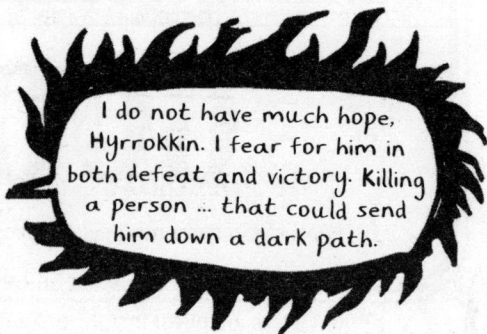

I do not have much hope, Hyrrokkin. I fear for him in both defeat and victory. Killing a person ... that could send him down a dark path.

I'd heard enough.

Back upstairs, I indulged in an important mortal ritual called lying on your bed listening to depressing music and contemplating the horrors of existence.

Or, in my case, the end of existence. Which was coming soon.

And I never even got my snack.

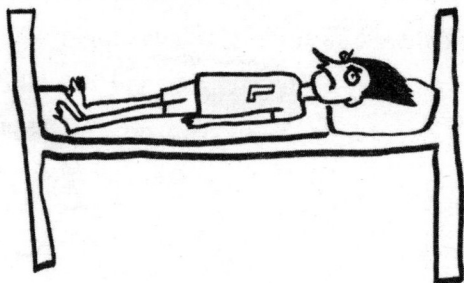

# Day Twenty-Two:
## Tuesday

## LOKI VIRTUE SCORE OR LVS:

# -600

### Points lost for needless cruelty to Vinir.

I woke up feeling oddly better. Mortal moods are strange because of chemicals in their fleshy brains. Whatever the cause, I felt a new sense of determination: I was going to defeat Vinir. I practised my spell before school and succeeded in turning a peach from a plump, fresh fruit to a pit surrounded by dust. My mind was not clouded by fears and distractions! For the very first time, I felt I could see PAST the duel.

I might ... win.

I walked to school with a spring in my step. It was a frosty morning so, naturally, Thor prowled beside me, alert for giants. I told him he was being ridiculous.

One day I'll be right about giants, and you'll be sorry.

Yes, I would be very sorry if you were right about something.

At lunch, Valerie and I sat together and tried a mortal drink called squash. This drink looks like fruit juice but its relationship to fruit is as distant as the blood kindred of a sausage and a turd. As I drank it, I had an unpleasant sensation in my gums. A dull ache. I did not like it. Regardless – this could not dampen my mood.

"I am feeling confident about my duel with Vinir," I told Valerie. "I will be victorious, and he will die! Is that not great?"

I expected a rapturous response from Valerie, perhaps something along the lines of...

I always believed in you. Your victory was inevitable.

But instead, she looked like this.

159

"Are you sure you can't talk your way out of this duel?" she asked.

"I've already told you, I will win!" I pointed out. Why was she still worrying?

"I know," she said. "It's just that I don't think Vinir deserves to die. Yes, he came here to kill you. And yes, he did a spell on everyone to make them think he was Alfie ... which he still hasn't taken off most people. But he's still a person."

A person who wants to kill MOI!

But, Loki. If you win, you'll be a murderer. I don't want you to be a **murderer**.

That word hit me with a thud. I wanted to yell at her that she was getting it all wrong. I was the victim here! Vinir challenged ME to a duel to the death!

But for some reason, instead of telling her she was being a terrible friend who knew nothing, I suggested we return to the lunch queue to see if we could persuade the kitchen staff to give us a second pudding each.

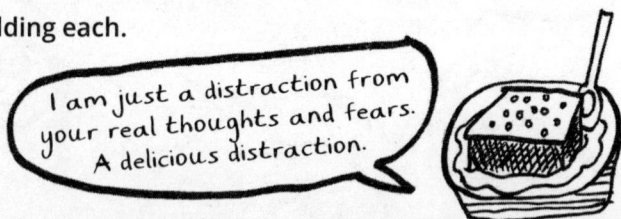

I am just a distraction from your real thoughts and fears. A delicious distraction.

In the evening, I practised my spell with Hyrrokkin again. This time on an apple. At my second (unsuccessful) attempt, Heimdall came into the kitchen.

EMPTY

Can someone explain why we are out of fruit and vegetables? I only did the big shop yesterday!

So my fake father cared more for the price of fruit than my very life!

"Heimdall, you're *not* helping," hissed Hyrrokkin. "Begin again, Loki."

I focused on the apple and performed the spell while picturing Vinir's stupid face. But instead of the clarity I felt before, my head was like a hornets' nest of irrelevant thoughts.

Please don't kill me!

I don't want you to be a murderer.

And the apple remained unhurt, taunting me.

YOU'RE GONNA DIE, LOSER.

# Day Twenty-Three:
## Wednesday

DIE!

My dreams were horrifying and, every time I saw Vinir in class or in the playground, those dreams haunted me afresh. It was ridiculous really. I couldn't perform the spell that would save my life because I was feeling guilty about trying to hurt someone who was TRYING TO MURDER ME!

Why can't I focus on murdering him right back?

A distraction came in the form of pain. In my mouth. Mortal bodies are ridiculous and unpleasant.

Luckily, it faded as a greater pain arose in my heart: Maths.

*mwahahahahahahaa!*

In the evening, Hyrrokkin sat me down with some weeds from the garden.

GOOD LUCK, Heimdall xx

But I merely stared at the plant matter. I knew I could not do the spell. I turned to Hyrrokkin. "When I try, I feel guilty about killing Vinir. Even though I know that is silly, because he wants to kill *me*!"

"Human hearts are complex things," said Hyrrokkin. She gave me a little half smile.

But I'm not human.

Chemically, you are right now. Use that. You could focus on another emotion so it drowns out the guilt for the length of the spell.

So I went up to my room to practise, grabbing some grapes on the way up. If I am to be a mighty magician, surely I cannot perform my spells on paltry weeds! I focused on how angry I was about my situation. I let the anger flood through me. And, what do you know, it WORKED.

1) Grapes    2) Sour grapes    3) Very, very dead grapes    4) Grape dust

Confusingly, after successfully destroying an entire bunch of grapes, I sank back on my bed and sobbed for an hour. Why was I weeping in the face of almost certain victory? It made no sense. I am not in favour of mortal emotions. I would like to file a petition to Odin.

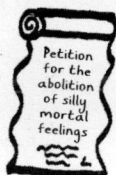

Petition for the abolition of silly mortal feelings

He never reads those, you know. !

Thor came up to see me before bed. "Loki, I was cleaning my hammer, and it started twitching in my hand. It KNOWS the giants are planning something."

We need to act.

FEED ME GIANTSSS!

"GO AWAY!" I yelled. Because why should I help Thor? It's not like he's offering to kill Vinir for me.

"But Loki ... this is important!" said Thor, sitting on the bed.

"Why does no one think *I* AM IMPORTANT?" I said. "Get out!"

"Wait, have you been crying?" he asked, looking at my face. "What's wrong?"

"Too late! You clearly don't care!"

Thor retreated, looking confused and upset, leaving me to my misery. On the plus side, I discovered some new miserable music to listen to as I thought dark thoughts.

> ! I wonder... Could you be starting to go through puberty? Mortal teenagers are often moody and brooding.

I AM NOT MOODY AND BROODING, I HAVE REAL PROBLEMS! AN ELF IS TRYING TO MURDER ME!!!!

5 minutes later...

BROODS MOODILY

# Day Twenty-Four:
## Thursday

There is a mortal expression that "Life kicks you when you're down". After today, I have decided it is one of the truest pieces of wisdom in all the nine worlds, for I awoke with an intense pain inside my mouth.

My tooth

It felt as though a giant was attempting to crack my head asunder, using my own teeth as weapons.

Hyrrokkin and Heimdall dragged me with great haste to a terrible place of unspeakable torture called The Dentist. Like all true supervillains, it takes the definite article, "the". Never "a" dentist.

GRRR

THE Dentist →

Rotten tooth

**Dentist:** a place where mortals go to pay someone to drill into their face.

And you're not even allowed to bite them when they stick their fingers in your mouth!

> But she was stealing my teeth!

Normally missing a good many school lessons would bring me joy, but there is no joy for one whose face is being drilled.

And *then* I had to go to school. What is my life? Perhaps death would be a mercy?

In Topic, we worked on our group project. Well, Valerie and Thor worked on it while Vinir and I exchanged barbs.

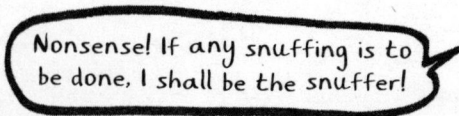

> Soon, your life will be snuffed out. Your doom approaches. Your end is in sight.

> Nonsense! If any snuffing is to be done, I shall be the snuffer!

At that, Valerie intervened. "Stop threatening each other and help," she said. She turned to Vinir. "Why *are* you doing all this?"

"Because I HATE him," he said, stabbing his finger in my direction.

"Lots of people hate Loki," chipped in Thor. "But all the others do not try to kill him. For example, my kindly wife, Sif, merely framed him for a crime he did not commit."

This isn't about mere, petty hate. It's about duty. I swore to avenge my father's honour. Blah blah Daddy this, blah blah Daddy that, blah blah vengeance, blah blah.

Mercifully, Valerie cut him off before my ears fell off with boredom.

"Changing your mind is a mature thing to do," said Valerie. "I changed my mind about Loki. I thought he was an evil alien at first. Then I thought he was an evil god. But now I like him."

I shimmied my shoulders in glee. "See! Be more Valerie!"

Vinir ignored me and looked at Valerie as though she had suggested jumping off a cliff without a flying machine.

Changing your mind is WEAK. It is dishonourable! My father would never forgive me.

By this point, Vinir was talking at considerable volume, so the teacher told us to sit down, pipe down and get on with our work or we'd get a detention.

An EXTRA one in your case, Liam.

So we did as she said.

I did my spell again tonight. I didn't even cry. Well, OK, only once.

! Twice.

OK, but the important thing is that I STOPPED crying. So ... progress?

# Day Twenty-Five:
## Friday

Due to my dental issues, detention was postponed to
today. It was to be the last one, and our decorations
were nearly ready. If I say so myself, our work was
most impressive.

> What do you mean "if I say so myself"? When
> do you ever NOT say so yourself?

!

Fine, you got me. But look at them! Glorious!

This was the first time I had ever, in my many thousands of years, completed a project.

Can I get a gold star please?

! As an incorporeal being, I cannot peel stickers off their backing. But I believe you should get some virtue points.

No stickers?

Alas, Georgina poured iced water on my warm and fuzzy mood.

"Now detention's ending, I don't need to talk to you any more," she said.

I should have felt jubilant that detention was ending, but after Georgina's words, I felt this:

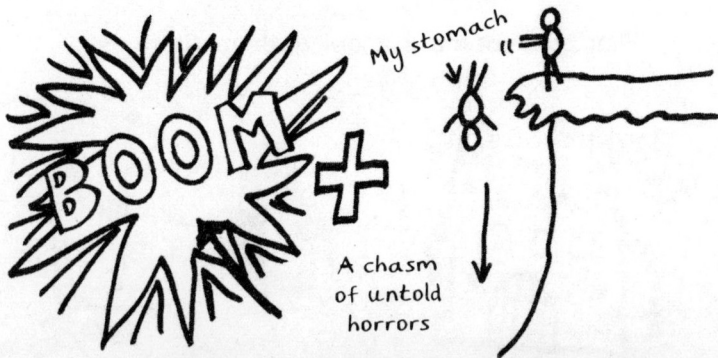

BOOM +

My stomach

A chasm of untold horrors

Even after all this time together, it seemed she had not forgiven me. As we packed up the leftover cardboard, I decided I would apologize properly, so she would have no choice but to forgive me.

(Well, as Georgina packed it up and I watched.)

> Georgina, I want you to know I am sorry for... I forget what I did to make you angry in the first place, but I am sorry. Please forgive me so we can be friends?

An excellent apology. I even said please!

> You got me into the biggest trouble of my life, AND I've not been riding since, AND I'm not sure my parents will ever trust me again. Does that refresh your memory?

"Oh, good, thank you, that's very helpful. Yes, I apologize for" – I waved my arms – "all of the above. NOW are we friends?"

"No," said Georgina, and turned away from me.

We sat in silence until the end of detention when the mortals Kris and Elsa came and shooed us out of the hall because they had to prepare everything for the fair. Georgina left without a backwards glance, but I followed her outside to discover her entire family had come to pick her up in a large and shiny car. Humph! Hyrrokkin and Heimdall make me walk like a peasant!

"Hi, Daddy," said Georgina, as she got into the back seat of the car.

Her father made a gruff noise.

Georgina turned her face as she got in and I could see that she was trying not to cry.

Perhaps she was crying with happiness because she had such a handsome father who owned such a luxurious car? I could not ponder long. I had work to do. I transformed myself and hitched a ride...

A totally ordinary woodlouse

Seatbelts!

For all the time I had spent with Georgina, I still could not understand why she cared so much about the opinion of her parents. This seemed like a good opportunity to untangle that mystery.

As the car drove off, Georgina's mother looked back at her. "Now that detention is over, no more of that Liam boy, OK?"

Georgina shook her head a little more forcefully than I liked. "No, Mummy, definitely not."

Her mother nodded. "Good. Your brothers look up to you, and we raised you to be better than that. Just because Liam's a bad influence, that doesn't mean you should listen to him, you hear me? Stay away from that boy."

Who, me?

"I promise. I will never speak to him again. I really won't. I don't want to."

Ouch. She's serious.

Her mother gave a slight nod. "Good. I love you, and I know you won't do anything like this again."

"No, Mummy."

"You can have your phone back now but you are not allowed back to the stables yet," her mum added, passing the phone back.

I watched Georgina with my little insect eyes as they drove on in silence. She looked so very sad.

Did I do that?

No, it was her tyrannical parents!

Well, I knew just how to cheer her up. With a sincere and – more importantly – stylish apology dance!

While Georgina and her parents had dinner, I scuttled upstairs to wait. It took so long I eventually fell asleep in Georgina's bedroom and only awoke as she called down to say goodnight, all ready for bed.

> Goodnight, Daddy! Goodnight, Mummy! Goodnight, everyone!

Her mother came into her room and gave her a little hug and kiss goodnight. All was forgiven, clearly. Which meant this was the perfect moment for my apology, with all the consequences of my actions now erased by her mother's warm embrace.

Just as Georgina closed the door, I transformed.

Without further ado, I began my song and dance. It was a riff on the one Sif performed for me to apologize for framing me for stealing Thor's hammer. Only my dance had extra flair and grace because it's me.

177

"What are you doing here?" she hissed, after going to the door and checking there was no one nearby.

"Apologizing, of course," I said. "I refer you to my highly moving performance!"

"Out of all the weird and creepy things you've ever done, this is the weirdest and creepiest," said Georgina, keeping her voice as low as her horror allowed.

Get out! If my parents find you here I'll be in even worse trouble than before.

Obviously I needed to explain my apology further, so I obeyed her instructions in such a way that I could continue this conversation.

Oh no. What did you do?                                    !

I might have slightly transformed her into a mouse.

SLIGHTLY?                                                  !

Entirely.

179

FLAP   FLAP

SQUEAK!

◇◇◇◇◇◇◇◇◇◇◇◇◇◇◇◇◇◇◇◇◇◇◇◇◇◇◇◇◇◇◇◇◇◇◇◇◇◇◇◇◇◇◇◇◇◇◇◇◇◇◇◇◇◇◇◇◇◇◇
! **Oh. Oh no. No no no.**
◇◇◇◇◇◇◇◇◇◇◇◇◇◇◇◇◇◇◇◇◇◇◇◇◇◇◇◇◇◇◇◇◇◇◇◇◇◇◇◇◇◇◇◇◇◇◇◇◇◇◇◇◇◇◇◇◇◇◇

Technically I obeyed her instructions – I left her bedroom!

So off I flew. I didn't have a plan and before I knew it, I was at school. Flying in through a window, I landed in the hall, which was all prepared for the fair the next day. Perhaps having a visual reminder of what wonderful work we had created together would help Georgina to be more open to my continued apology.

Except, when I transformed her back into her true shape, she seemed less than enthused by the whole situation.

So, as well as sneaking into my bedroom at night, you think KIDNAPPING me is a good way to apologize?

It's not like that!

So often my intentions are taken the wrong way. It is my curse.

TAKE ME BACK!

I knew that I only needed to explain to her why she was wrong, and why she should forgive me, and our friendship would be so beautiful that people would talk of it through the ages.

PSYCH 101
The eternal friendship of Loki and Georgina

Unfortunately I was interrupted by heavy footsteps clomping into the hall.

"*Hide,*" I hissed at Georgina.

We hid behind the cardboard ice palace and I peeked around the edge.

Into the hall stomped...

All is nearly prepared for the fair! Our victory is near!

As we hid, I had a horrifying thought.

"Oh no," I said. "This is terrible. It means..."

"... we are probably going to die?" finished Georgina.

I shook my head. "Worse."

"*Worse?*"

"It means Thor was right," I said. "It WAS giants."

Georgina's eyes widened. "Wait, Thor was telling you the whole time something was going on with the giants and you ignored him?"

"In my defence—"

At that moment, I felt a lurching sensation as the cardboard that I was leaning against gave way under me.

Instinct took over and I transformed Georgina and myself into the first forms I could think of.

"Sorry!" I said, in my new voice. "We are just dinner ladies who got locked in the school after work."

Georgina caught on quickly. "Please don't hurt us," she added.

"Dinner ladies? Does that mean we can eat them?" said Captain Icebeard.

"We've *talked* about this," hissed General Glacier. "Don't make me tap the sign."

Not being eaten was good, but what WOULD they do with us? I never found out because a window in the hall exploded.

I did not see THAT coming.

**Neither did I. And I am versed in prophecies both ancient and modern.**

As we swooped through the sky, I turned Georgina and myself back into our true forms. Our dinner lady uniforms were not aerodynamic.

This is weird, right?

HUH?

A rare case of me being lost for words

When Vinir set us down, Georgina turned on me. "You kidnapped me! You turned me into a mouse AND a dinner lady without asking! And you nearly got me eaten by giants! You are so messed up!"

Before I could defend myself, she turned to Vinir. "Thank you for rescuing us. Can you get me home before my parents notice I'm gone?"

I blinked. This was a very odd thing to be concerned about after being snatched from the jaws of death.

> Why do you care what your parents think? They're merely the ones who spawned you.

> Just because YOU think parents are ornamental, doesn't make it true. I'm not a god who doesn't care about anyone. They're my mum and dad and I love them — and they're so disappointed in me.

Georgina looked down and bit her lip.

"I'm sorry," I said, feeling a clench in my abdomen region at the sight of her face.

"Are you? Sorry people don't keep doing bad things over and over again," she said. "I still haven't forgotten how you mind-controlled everyone, you know."

"Ah, I was rather hoping you had," I said. Mortals have such long memories for people with such short lives. Or perhaps it is *because* they have short lives? The shorter the life, the easier it is to keep it all in your head?

> You're just too much. I can't actually be angry with you because you're so ridiculous I want to laugh.

Well *that* felt like progress.

"We're still not friends, though," she added, and I deflated as the painful pin of rejection pierced my heart.

"Take me home, please."

she asked Vinir, who had been watching in silence, and they flew away.

When Vinir caught up with me on my way home, I demanded to know how he'd found us at the school.

> Simple.

> PLUCK!

> GASP

It was a tiny metal button that I hadn't noticed was even there. Perhaps Hyrrokkin is right and I SHOULD wash behind my ears more?

"Magical tracker," he explained. "Obviously I needed to observe your every move in case you ran away and broke our bargain."

You were spying on me?

OF COURSE I spied on you. You proudly call yourself a liar, and have a reputation as the most untrustworthy of the Aesir!

OK, that was fair.

"One thing I don't understand," I said, as we stood in the moonlight outside my front door. "And, as a supremely clever god, this is a rare occurrence. But ... if you want to kill me anyway, why bother rescuing me?"

Vinir bowed his head. "I could not let them hurt you."

For a moment, I was touched, until he raised his head again and added:

I could not let the giants kill you because destiny demands I do that myself.

With that, he turned and walked away.

"Where have you been?" asked Heimdall when I went inside.

"Getting kidnapped by giants," I said. "And rescued by Vinir. It's been *quite* the evening."

Thor's pretty little face lit up and I knew what was coming next.

I closed my eyes. I shall not recount what happened next.

! **You have to. You must.**

Do you mean, in order for you to accurately calculate my virtue points?

! **No, because it sounds like it was funny.**

I really HAVE been a bad influence on you. Very well.

Then we got on to less humiliating but more serious matters: what exactly the giants were planning. And how to stop them.

*Heimdall's notes and my helpful annotations*

## What we know
These four giants are planning to do something on the day of the fair.

*Heimdall can't draw*

## What they are planning involves the school

*Probably because I go to that school.*

*It's my school too! – Thor*

*Heimdall is a fart head who knows nothing.*

## What we don't know
What they are planning to do at the fair.

While I helped Heimdall get up to speed, Hyrrokkin was frowning over a book. Eventually she said, "Something like this has happened before..."

She shut the book and explained that there was a legend of a god spending time on Midgard a few thousand years ago. Their presence here resulted in the barrier between the worlds becoming thinner.

Ancient Tales of Ancient Gods

"Perhaps whatever the giants are planning is easier because you and Thor have spent months in that school, making the world walls thinner," she finished.

"Clearly an indication that we should no longer go to school, for the safety of the mortal realms," I offered selflessly.

"Nice try," said Hyrrokkin. "Once the barriers have become weaker, they're stuck like that. You won't make it better by bunking off."

TURDS.

"Now. Off to bed," said Heimdall. "Your mortal bodies need sleep, and you can make plans tomorrow."

But before bed, I saw a message from Georgina.
Joy of joys! I was forgiven!

> I still hate you. But we need to stop whatever the giants have planned. My parents are going to be at the fair. The whole school will. We need to stop them. Speak tomorrow.

What I'm taking from this is that she wants to speak to me!

! **And she hates you.**

Spotted that bit, did you?

# Day Twenty-Six:
## Saturday

In the morning I woke up to roughly one million shouty messages from Valerie.

> LOKI! VINIR TOLD ME EVERYTHING! I'M SO GLAD YOU AND GEORGINA ARE SAFE!

> I'M GOING TO SEE HER RIGHT NOW.

> ARE YOU OK?

> In spite of merely being an afterthought to you while you rush to Georgina's side, yes I am.

195

> Don't be silly, I knew YOU'D be OK. You're always OK.

I mean, I AM superbly awesome, I suppose.

> Anyway. Since Vinir saved you … I wonder if you two CAN make peace?

I'd rather eat an entire fresh dog turd.

I was feeling light-headed. Breakfast would solve that. If you don't feed mortal bodies at frequent intervals, they begin to lose their faculties and act erratically. Especially Thor. You don't want to see him when he's HANGRY.

Everyone except Heimdall was already up and out. Thor was walking Fido – mostly because Heimdall insisted that he went so he didn't "do anything stupid" in terms of attacking the giants without a proper plan – and Hyrrokkin had gone to the shops to buy cakes she could pass off as her own.

WE ARE LIARS.

As I ate my toast, I got a text from Valerie.

196

Meet me and Georgina at the school. We need
to look for clues about the giants' plan.

Are you sure she'll put up
with spending time with me?

She's willing to do it to save the world.

Basically she's forgiven me then?

No.

We arranged to meet outside school. Heimdall
gave me a copy of Odin's magical skeleton key and
said to call if we needed any help. When we met...

"Why is *he* here?" I hissed to Valerie.

Valerie whispered, "I thought this would be the perfect opportunity for you two to work together and make peace!"

After we entered the school using our magical key, Valerie and Georgina went off in the opposite direction to look for clues, leaving me alone with Vinir.

"I am SO sorry, my princeling," I said, with an extra-sarcastic bow. Sarcasm might not be the height of wit but it's one of the big five!

"Why *are* you helping?" I asked. I drew back my shoulders. "Not that I need your help. I have defeated the Frost Giants MANY times without your aid."

"Firstly, as I have told you, it is my destiny to kill you myself," said Vinir, as we walked down a corridor looking about for evidence of what the giants might be up to. "But, as you so often seem to forget, this is not just about you. These mortals do not deserve whatever the giants have planned. They are weak and vulnerable, like kittens."

"I dare you to say that to their faces," I said, rather liking the idea of how Valerie and Georgina would react to being called kittenish.

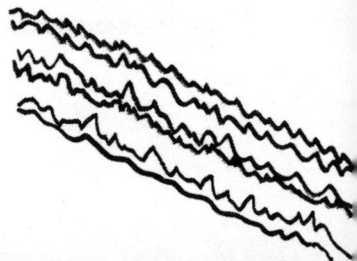

Vinir snorted and went on. "Nor do your guardians on this plane deserve to freeze on this Earth, nor Thor, with whom I have no quarrel. He seems an honourable person."

I made a face. Of COURSE Vinir thought Thor was amazing. He'd probably been giving him The Look while I wasn't looking.

Then I heard my conscience.

> Careful. Remember what happened last time you got jealous of everyone admiring Thor?

> OK, OK, so I lost control and turned into a giant wolf and tried to kill Thor, one time, I get it. I shall dial down the jealousy.

Honestly, life was SO much easier before I grew a conscience. Much more peaceful!

**! So peaceful you ended up getting thrown out of Asgard.**

Peaceful *inside* I mean.

We wandered into the hall. Everything seemed unremarkable and lacking in evidence of giant behaviour.

Perfectly innocent cardboard decorations

Normal tables

I was starting to think that we would never find anything when Georgina called me over and pointed to one of my cardboard masterpieces. Valerie was staring at the animal's bottom. Odd girl.

Well, that DEFINITELY wasn't there when I finished painting it.

It was just a single letter, so meant nothing alone. "There might be more. Check the other sculptures," I commanded.

"Calling these items 'sculptures' is perhaps a *slight* exaggeration," said Vinir.

"You try making a classical sculpture out of cardboard, poster paints and glue sticks," I said.

Vinir just raised an eyebrow. I hate him. How dare he go around using his eyebrows as weapons of emotional cruelty?

Luckily he went off to check a penguin, so I didn't have to look at his face any more.

We gathered to scroll through the pictures Valerie had taken of the various runes. "What does it all spell out?" asked Georgina. "I don't speak Viking."

"These aren't actually Viking runes," said Valerie. "They're older than that. From the Elder Futhark."

"How do you know that?" I asked, impressed.

"I've been studying the Norse myths and Viking culture since you arrived," said Valerie. "So, can you read them?"

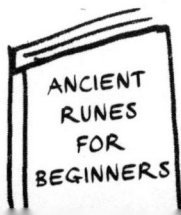

I nodded. "Yes, obviously, I'm exceptionally brilliant."

> **!** **Correction: you are not exceptionally brilliant. All gods have been taught the runes by Odin.**

However, even my brilliance was not enough. The jumble of runes we had collected could be combined to form *so many* words. The idea of crawling through them all filled my soul with horrifying tedium.

Georgina's eyes lit up at this. "I have a program we can use for that!"

Valerie seemed equally excited and trotted off with Georgina to the I.T. room, promising they'd be back soon.

While we waited for them, Vinir took some spare cardboard, some paint and a glue stick from one of the tables. Then, without breaking eye contact, he created an abstract sculpture of heartbreaking beauty.

You laid down the challenge. I cannot but answer.

In that moment I hated him with every single fibre of my being. Valerie's suggestion of talking him out of the duel was silly. He needed a good being killed.

But that would make me a killer.

I'm a trickster, a prankster, a joker. I'm NOT a killer. After all, there's nothing witty about killing, is there?

Shortly, Valerie and Georgina came back, bubbling with excitement.

"My program showed what all the possible combinations of those runes could be," said Georgina.

"I've got the results on my phone," said Valerie, passing it to me.

I scrolled down and down until one unusual word jumped out at me – a giantish word meaning "to make real". I'd seen it in a spell before – in one of Hyrrokkin's spell books. But what did it do?

I closed my eyes to focus, allowing the memory to come flooding up from wherever I store memories when I'm not repressing them to avoid feeling things. I knew what the Frost Giant spell was for. And it wasn't for making sure everyone at the winter fair had a very nice time.

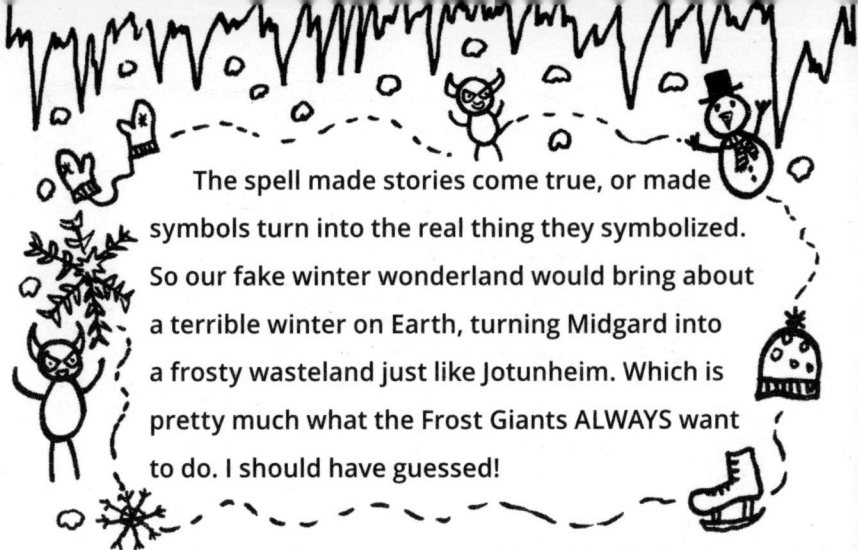

The spell made stories come true, or made symbols turn into the real thing they symbolized. So our fake winter wonderland would bring about a terrible winter on Earth, turning Midgard into a frosty wasteland just like Jotunheim. Which is pretty much what the Frost Giants ALWAYS want to do. I should have guessed!

A short while later, we formed a council of war at a nearby cafe: Valerie, Georgina, Vinir and me, as well as Thor, Heimdall and Hyrrokkin, who brought the relevant spell book.

My fake parents bought us all a hot chocolate with marshmallows and a chocolate flake each, which is the main reason I invited them, aside from the spell book.

! **You should respect them more.**

I will never respect anyone as much as I respect hot chocolate.

I brought everyone up to speed about the giants' spell by drawing on the tablecloth that the cafe conveniently provided for the purpose.

"And," I finished, "we know the giants will be at the fair because the spell requires the one who casts it to be close to the objects they plan to transform."

Hyrrokkin seemed very touched that I remembered such a detail from one of the spells in her book.

Well done, Loki.

"Don't expect me to remember any more details," I said. Setting low expectations in other people's minds is helpful – that way any small act of goodness seems more exaggerated.

> ! SO YOU'RE DOING THAT ON PURPOSE, ARE YOU? That's it, minus points!

The question remained: how would we STOP the giants' spell?

Hmmm...

208

209

I was about to dismiss this vague, shapeless idea but it happened to give me another, brilliant idea.

"Can you edit spells? Take a spell that's supposed to be for one thing and make it for another?"

Hyrrokkin nodded. "Yes. You can combine two spells. Which spell did you have in mind?"

The spell I've been practising!

Oh! That could work. If you alter the words slightly, and add a new gesture, yes!

"What are you all talking about?" said Thor, looking confused. Or rather, looking Thor.

Valerie had been taking notes, and she turned them around so Thor could see.

Life force

VS

Spell energy

"The spell Loki and Vinir are using in their duel sucks the life out of someone," Valerie explained. "So the edited version, instead of sucking the life out of a person, would suck the energy out of a spell."

"EXACTLY, Valerie Kerry, wisest among mortals!" Hyrrokkin slapped Valerie on the back so hard she dropped her pencil.

Vinir, Hyrrokkin, Heimdall and I huddled together and worked through the details, while Thor polished his hammer and sulked in the corner, and Valerie and Georgina talked. I half listened.

Now detention's over, can you go riding?

Not yet. My parents are still acting like they don't trust me.

"I won't go to the stables until you're allowed back," said Valerie.

"No, you *have* to go. You have to look after Rusty and give him apples for me."

"Do you think they'll relax soon?" asked Valerie.

Miss u, Georgina.

"Relax? My parents? They haven't relaxed once in their entire lives. Even when they were babies, I bet my dad wore tailored nappies. My mum could probably do her own braids before she could walk because it was the responsible and grown-up thing to do." Georgina sighed and put her face in her hands. "I wish none of this had happened."

I felt uncomfortable listening to that. A kind of hot stabbing in my chest area.

! Guilt?

Or maybe I drank my hot chocolate too quickly?

# Day Twenty-Seven:
## Sunday

### LOKI VIRTUE SCORE OR LVS:

# -800

**50 points lost for setting low expectations on purpose.**

I woke up knowing that today might be my last chance to prove I can be a Good God. So I was going to do something terrifying.

**What are you planning?**                                    !

Aren't you supposed to have the wisdom of Odin? You clearly don't have his patience.

After breakfast we all got dressed for the fair. Some of us got more dressed than others.

HAHAHAHA

Ho ho
Heimdall

Heimdall looked very hilarious,
which cheered me up.

The plan was to meet the others
at school before the fair began. We
had to act as though nothing was out
of the ordinary, so that the giants wouldn't
know that we knew what they had planned.

Stop laughing at me, Loki!

Just doing what they're
supposed to be doing

Everything's normal

Even when an apocalypse is looming, you cannot
get between Valerie and Georgina and doing their
schoolwork. It didn't take them long, however, as
most parents had walked. Something we did not
factor into our business plan, alas.

I spent the time doing what I would naturally do
on any other day: insulting my enemy.

Shouldn't you be
assisting your boss,
Little Helper?

214

We knew the giants would be at the fair, so we kept an eye out for anyone acting shiftily.

Could it be them?          Or them?

Hyrrokkin set up her cake stall. She'd done a convincing job of making the cakes look homemade. I suspect she did violence to those poor baked goods to ensure they had an amateurish look.

OH WOE, WE ARE BRUISED.

Heimdall sat upon his Santa throne and adjusted his beard.

Thor set up his goalie stand and adjusted his wedgie.

I pretended to do a few little touch-ups with paint on my sculptures so no one would tell me to do anything *actually* useful.

Hyrrokkin and Heimdall's tedious mortal friends waved from their tombola stall.

"We should get the mortals out before they notice anything strange," said Hyrrokkin, looking worried.

"I'll sort that out when the time comes," said Heimdall.

Then the hordes descended.

! Wait. The giants attacked? Just like that?

No, but the staff let all the adults and children into the fair, and it was like being attacked by a wall of screaming and chaos.

Please imagine a drawing of hundreds of people here. Loki doesn't have the time to draw crowd scenes.

Amid the crowd, I saw THEM. The people I would have to prostrate myself before and face their wrath.

What? Odin and his wife Frigg were not at the fair, were they?

Georgina's parents...

216

## Oh.                                               !

Georgina and her parents were chatting to some other adults, who did not interest me, but I waited until they had finished, for that is what a Good God does. And this might have been my last chance to prove that is what I am.

Excuse me, could I say a few words, Mrs Olowo?

Is this the infamous Liam?

Georgina nodded, giving me death stares and mouthing, "*WHAT ARE YOU DOING?*"

"I wanted you both to know that Georgina had nothing to do with the fire alarm incident. She was telling you the truth. It's all my fault."

I decided that words were not enough to express my contrition, so I prostrated myself upon the floor.

Utter disbelief

217

Very sticky

Instant regret

Forgive me, Georgina.

"I let you take the blame with your parents," I went on. My little mortal heart was hammering like I was in physical danger. How odd. "I was a coward who did not want to face the full wrath of the teachers alone. I let your parents think you had been bad and you are good. Mostly."

As I gave my speech, I heard Georgina's mother whisper, "That boy is *really* not OK, is he?" But at the end she added in a louder voice:

Thank you for telling us, Liam.

Georgina shot me a look as though to say GO AWAY NOW. So I went away. But obviously I listened in on the remainder of the conversation.

Her mother smiled. "As long as you do all your homework after the fair."

"YAY!" Georgina hugged her mum and dad both at once. "Shall we go home now so I can do it?"

"Are you sure?" asked her mother. "You don't want to stay and enjoy the fair?"

Georgina shook her head and led her parents

away to safety before anything unnatural began to happen.

As they left, Georgina glanced back at me. While she didn't say anything, her face showed that, perhaps, just perhaps, she was wishing for my death slightly less?

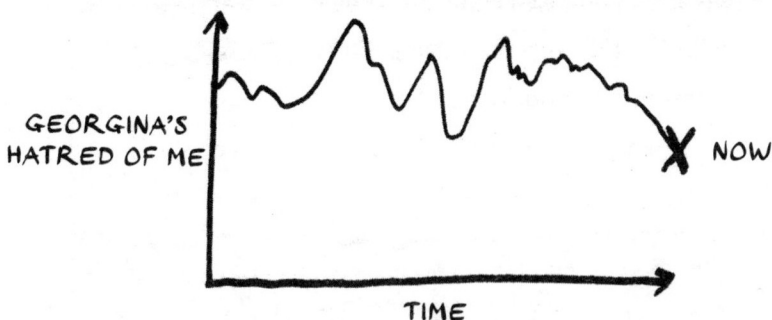

GEORGINA'S HATRED OF ME | NOW

TIME

But I couldn't bask in this wondrous moment, for the giants could begin their spell at any second. I had to be ready. I spent a few minutes reminding myself of the spell-draining spell, then looked around to check that everyone else was ready.

Hyrrokkin and Heimdall were looking out for anyone behaving suspiciously.

No, she always looks that nervous.

Please don't have a tantrum.

220

Thor was glancing around less subtly, but people kept kicking footballs at him, which (thankfully) prevented him from staring constantly. That god would make the worst spy in history. Hard to believe he's sneaky Odin's son sometimes.

Then I spotted four mortals behaving suspiciously. Two adults and two children. They were standing behind a stall with their arms out, clearly saying something, but not to each other...

I know those mortals! EXCEPT ... they were not mortals at all, were they?

(Words too quiet to hear but if they're not spell words then I'll eat a pie made of hair!)

Hyrrokkin and Heimdall's friends Elsa and Kris and their children are ACTUALLY GIANTS IN DISGUISE!

I texted Hyrrokkin at her station behind the cake stall. Her eyes flared with surprise. But there was no time to talk. I nodded across the hall to Vinir, who was waiting for my signal.

We began our counterspell.

We couldn't have "Elsa and Kris" notice the counterspell too soon, or they'd have a chance to foil it. But Valerie, possibly the smartest mortal I know, started walking around the hall, whispering in people's ears. I caught the words "Free cake" as she pointed to the tombola stall.

Humans swarmed around the stall like flies around a juicy poo. Kris and Elsa continued the spell while their "children" stopped to fend off the hungry mortals.

Stick figures = a lazy god's hack to drawing crowd scenes

Cake-hungry mortals

222

As the Frost Giants' spell took hold, the air grew chill. Ice glistened on the windowpanes. The windows slammed open, snow began to fall and the wind whipped around us.

The mortals in the hall started to notice that something was wrong.

Time for Heimdall's part of the plan to kick in.

Ho! Ho! Ho! Join me in the playground for **FREE PRESENTS!**

"Oh my god!" screamed Valerie, at a volume that even some giants could barely muster. "FREE PRESENTS!" She ran after him to set an example to everyone else. They didn't need much encouragement.

223

The stampeding horde reminded me of a nature documentary that Hyrrokkin made me watch, where wildebeests chase across the plains of ... somewhere or other. Only these feral beasts wanted FREE THINGS.

As the mortals left, the giants' spell grew in strength. Our counterspell couldn't hold it back and everything Georgina and I had made out of flimsy cardboard became real. The animals shook and snorted and howled with life. The wobbly painted palace became a vast and shining edifice, studded with diamond garlands of sharp icicles hanging from the eaves. Finally, the giants shook off their mortal forms, pretence dissolving into glorious triumph.

Bravely performing counterspell in the face of danger →

Waving hammer for no reason

Somebody screamed.

You?                                    !

Maybe.

The giants fled, leaving behind only scattered cardboard and the occasional snowflake and ball of polar bear fur.

We also made a hasty exit before any of the fairgoers returned from mobbing Heimdall for presents and saw the state of the hall. As we retreated, Valerie returned from shepherding mortals away from danger and ran up to me in the corridor.

You did it!

I found myself falling in step with the elf as all of us walked oh-so-unsuspiciously towards the exit.

"So," Vinir said, "tomorrow we are set to duel."

Oh good. I was already feeling greatly fatigued from the spell and definitely needed an additional layer of paralysing dread at my imminent demise.

"If you are willing," Vinir went on, "I say we should *not* duel tomorrow."

Now we had fought side by side, had he forgiven me? Was I safe? Was I going to live after all?

Unfortunately he hadn't finished.

"That was a gruelling spell," he said. "Since you are a less experienced magician than me, I will give you longer to recover. We shall duel on Tuesday instead. But you fought well, my enemy," he added, glancing at me with the slightest of half smiles. A smile like a knife, like a crescent moon in the darkest night.

As I looked at his face, I knew I couldn't kill him. I hated him, sure, from his irritatingly silky hair to the tips of his no doubt annoyingly beautiful toes. But the idea of taking my wand and drawing the life out of him felt wrong – especially as he looked so sad.

"Thank you," was all I could say, when what I *wanted* to say was:

This is so stupid! We don't have to do this — why are we doing this? I don't want to do this!

We had saved the mortal realms. I should have felt elated. But the duel hung in the air above me.

The day after tomorrow, I was going to die.

The spell had drained me like a wineskin at a feast and, as soon as we arrived home, I curled up on my bed and pulled the blankets over my head.

Alas, my peace was disturbed when Hyrrokkin knocked on the door and came to sit on the corner of my bed.

"Tell me what is wrong," she said quietly.

I came out reluctantly from under the blankets. Feeling their softness against my face gave me

a momentary sense of safety, but they could not protect me.

"I'm going to lose the duel," I said.

"You can perform the spell successfully," she said, knotting her thick eyebrows in concern. "So why are you so certain you shall lose?"

"I'm proud that you cannot kill him because your heart is too good," she said.

But my heart did not feel good. It felt terrified.

"I believe you will find a solution," said Hyrrokkin. "You are the trickster god, after all. You have never met a trap from which you cannot escape!"

I pulled back to look at her. "Are you telling me to be *more* of a trickster?"

Hyrrokkin held up a finger. "Not in general. But, on this one occasion, perhaps it is best. You're not a fighter – I know that – but I have faith that you can wriggle out of this."

I felt a little better after that. I AM a trickster. I can trick Vinir into not killing me. Somehow.

But as I went to sleep that night, all I could think about was that tomorrow might be my last full day on Earth. If I die in the duel, that's it. I won't be a Good God, I will only be whatever I have been up until now... I won't be able to prove everyone wrong.

And, hey, that IS something worth living for!

OMG ARGH OMG!

I'm right, you're wrong.

# Day Twenty-Eight:
## Monday

```
LOKI VIRTUE SCORE OR LVS:

-300

500 points added for apologizing
properly. Genuine moral progress!
```

At breakfast, Hyrrokkin asked me about the duel.
I was about to tell her that I was still very afraid but,
when I saw the worry on her face, other words came
out. I didn't lie, exactly. I merely took the truth and
gave it a little hat.

Little
hat

"Oh, didn't I tell you? Vinir's called off the duel
today," I said, in my most cheerful voice.

Truth

Technically true – even the diary cannot argue with
the fact that Vinir HAD called off today's duel. I simply
didn't mention tomorrow's...

My family's reaction was mixed.

Excellent! I knew you would weasel your way out of it!

Oh, what a relief!

Hmmm...

Heimdall and Thor were thrilled. Thor even did a celebratory fart on my head.

Hyrrokkin was more sceptical.

"Why didn't you tell me last night? How did you trick him into cancelling the duel?" she asked. "Why haven't you bragged about how you did it?"

I gave her a guilty look and then yawned dramatically. "It's because I persuaded him to turn our duel into an online gaming battle and I stayed up all night playing video games. Sorry."

"Do elves play video games?" Hyrrokkin frowned deeply.

To avoid further questions, I swiftly and skilfully changed the subject. "So, Kris and Elsa and their so-called children were Frost Giants all along! What a shock that nobody could have anticipated."

Thor merely growled at this.

"I can't believe our first mortal friends turned out to be Frost Giants in disguise!" said Heimdall, toying with his breakfast.

"Well, I'm glad I never helped them with the tombola at least," said Hyrrokkin, looking grim. "I should have realized they were the giants. It was Elsa and Kris who suggested the winter fair theme!"

"The fault is mine. I should have trusted my instincts and insisted," said Thor. "My hammer twitched when they were around!"

TOLD YOU SO.

"And I should not have insisted Thor was being ridiculous," I said, keen to keep away from the thorny topic of Vinir, and Hyrrokkin's face of worried scepticism.

Admitting Thor was right? Are you feeling all right, son?

Apparently that was a step too far. Hyrrokkin leaned towards me. "Loki, tell me honestly, what happened with Vinir?"

I looked at the clock in an exaggerated fashion.

235

U looking at me, mate?

"Well, isn't that a shame, I have to go to school now."

> **Loki, you should have told them the truth.**
> **Why were you lying about the duel?**

I'm a liar, it's what I do!

> **It's not that.**

OK, it's not. I just... I don't want to tell them I can't come up with anything to persuade Vinir to cancel our duel properly. I don't want to fail. I don't want to be ... inadequate.

> **Do you want to die in an unwinnable duel?**

I'll think of something. I always do.

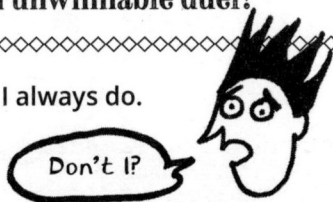

Don't I?

In assembly, the head teacher apologized for events at the school fair. Although Heimdall had cleared the hall with his offer of free presents, a few mortals DID see what happened through the window.

"Unfortunately, the air-conditioning system that we had fitted recently malfunctioned, leading to ice forming over the windows," the head told everyone. "Then it seems a number of animals must have escaped from the local zoo. Again."

That zoo has a serious problem with security. First the lion and those snakes...

And no one ever explained why there was a giant wolf on stage for the school play.

At break, I told Valerie about the duel being called off due to the epic video-game marathon. She gave me a rib-crushing hug and told me that she knew I'd find a way out.

I tried to absorb her confidence, but sadly mortal emotions, while somewhat catching, do not pass through the skin.

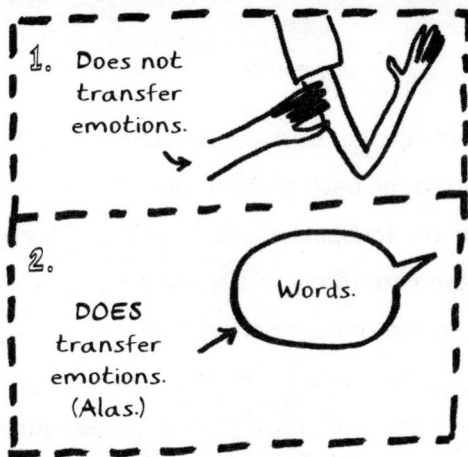

1. Does not transfer emotions.

2. DOES transfer emotions. (Alas.)

Words.

What she said next, however, sucked any *positive* feelings out of me.

"I can't wait to tell Vinir that I'm glad that you've resolved your differences peacefully using computer games!"

"Better not mention it," I said hurriedly. "He's a sore loser."

"Oh, of course," said Valerie, and promised not to mention it to Vinir.

Phew, one bullet dodged. Unfortunately...

VALERIE BLABBING TO VINIR

THE ACTUAL DUEL

In lessons, I watched Vinir. What *would* persuade him to change his mind? Perhaps I could run now?

Had he put another bug on me? I felt behind my ears and all down the back of my neck. While there was nothing there, I suspected that if I ran, he'd find me.

At the end of the day, Valerie and Georgina were chatting by the coats. I went to join them. I was still wary around Georgina, but if I was going to die tomorrow, what did I have to fear from a mortal child?

> What if she still hates me? What if she doesn't want to be my friend?

> Turns out, even if you're going to die, these things are still terrifying. Mortal brains are badly built.

Luckily, she did not seem inclined to mock me for my bad character. Instead she mocked me for my lack of knowledge of mortal movies.

"So, Valerie was telling me that those friends of your parents who turned out to be the giants in disguise ... they were called Kris and Elsa. And their 'kids' were called Olaf and Anna ... and you didn't for a second think that might be a hint that they were Frost Giants?"

I wrinkled my nose. I did not see why this might provide any kind of clue as to their true identity. As far as I was concerned, they were perfectly ordinary mortal names.

I looked blankly at her.

"I haven't seen it either," said Valerie. "I thought it would just be about princesses."

# Day Twenty-Nine:
## Tuesday

## LOKI VIRTUE SCORE OR LVS:

# -400

**100 points lost for lying.**

It looked like any other day ...

Normal clouds

Normal sky

Normal birds

... but it was absolutely not. The duel was set for
after school, in the boys' toilets in the sports pavilion,

as no one ever went in there unless there was a sportsball match. Dying in a toilet. The glamour.

OI! RUDE!

I ate my breakfast on autopilot and nearly choked on some toast, which I had to admit did not feel like a good omen.

In class, the fear built inside me like powerful rushing water behind a dam, and I considered telling Valerie the truth. Perhaps she could help? Before I could do that, however, there was a knock on the door to our classroom.

Alfie's dad's here to see him.

I had almost forgotten that was Vinir's human name until he got up to leave. His face looked very serious. I mean, even more serious than the humourless creature usually looks.

Could it really be his ACTUAL murderous elf king father?

Shortly after, I excused myself to go to the toilet. Then I turned myself into a mouse. This I *had* to see.

Vinir was in reception with a stranger carrying what looked like some kind of flute. The stranger

looked human. But then, so do I. Well, when I'm not a mouse.

Then I realized the object he was carrying was NOT a flute.

A magical barrier formed around the two of them, and tiny mouse me, shielding all of us from view.

The stranger passed a hand across his face, magically revealing his true elven self. I didn't recognize him but surely he had to be ...

243

# VOLUND!
### (Father of Vinir)

"That's better," he said. "Now, what are you doing here looking like THAT? Disgusting." He waved his wand and Vinir stood there in his true shape. Taller than I'd remembered. And luminously beautiful, curse him. How dare my deadly enemy go around looking like he'd spent hours in hair and make-up?

"I have come to avenge our family's honour, Father!" said Vinir, with a bow. "I had to do it in the form of a mortal, to make it a fair fight against a weaker opponent."

Volund inspected his immaculate nails, as though they were far more interesting than his equally immaculate son. "I have no idea what you are bleating about, boy."

"The god Loki insulted me in front of you at the feast!" said Vinir. His voice sounded pleading. "I have challenged him to a duel. I thought you'd be pleased."

244

"Oh, that." Volund waved his hand. "Loki is beneath me. A mere insect of a god."

Hey! How dare you! Also, technically I'm a MOUSE of a god right now.

Volund looked down his perfectly sloped nose at his son. "You should have cut him down with your magic then and there if you wanted to stand up to him. I've done worse to many for far, far less. Seeking a duel now is too little too late," snarled Volund. "I should have left you out for the wolves as an infant, for the dishonour you bring upon my name."

I suddenly felt a strong urge to slap him. But, as a mouse, that wouldn't be very effective.

"But Father, you said that an elf always protects his honour, and the honour of his family."

Their exchange was more lord and peasant than father and son, and I found myself looking away, as though I'd witnessed an act of violence.

Volund's face was a mask. And not one of those funny masks you wear for parties. His face was closed. A fortress.

↑
Damage caused: zero

"Duels are for elflings," he said, waving his elegant fingers in the air. "Mere children's games. I thought you had grown out of that."

"But—" said Vinir.

His father silenced him with a look.

> I have been thinking. In elven law, as my only son, you are my heir. You will be prince when I am gone.

Hope

Volund stopped in front of his son. "But I have decided."

> I have no son. You are a weakling, unworthy of the name Volundsson.

> What are you saying?

"For the good of the kingdom," said Volund, raising his hand and swiping it in a formal gesture I did not recognize. "I disown you. I will choose a new heir from among the worthy young elves of our realm."

246

And with that, the horrible old elf vanished.

Vinir sat down on a sofa by the door that was far
too small for his elf form and pulled his knees
up to his chest. He sat there slumped for
a moment before finally pulling himself
upright and getting out his wand.

247

This moment should have felt sweet. My enemy was brought low! Humiliated! Ashamed! I tried to summon a good gloat. But none would come. Behind him, I turned back into human form.

Perhaps sensing my handsome fabulousness, Vinir leaped to his feet and turned on me, holding out his wand.

I took a deep breath and expected to feel the wash of victory rush through me. But all I felt was ... I'm not sure. My chest felt large and painful, and my stomach hollow.

I heard a voice.

> You know what it is. You feel empathy.

"Look," I said. "I'm sorry. When I insulted you in front of your father, I didn't realize it was" – I waved at the window – "like that between you two. I should not have done that. I'm sorry."

"Stop trying to get out of our duel," spat Vinir. "Coward. You think you can buy me off with words?"

"No!" I said. "I don't want to fight you, that's absolutely true. But that's not why I'm saying this."

> I really am sorry.

**TRUTH ... shockingly ... detected.** !

> I'm as surprised as you, Diary.

"What do you care?" said Vinir. His anger had softened into mere distrust.

"Your father is *horrible* and I gave him ammunition to be even more horrible to you," I said. "So for what it's worth, I'm sorry." I reached out my hand as though to offer him some comfort, but I feared he would read it as a sneak attack, so I lowered my arm again and shrugged. "When I insult people, it's a game to me. Just a bit of fun to while away the tedium of eternity."

That is how it had always felt, at least. I had forever. The present was a game and I could always make something of myself tomorrow. But now I did not have tomorrow. I had to be good now, or never.

Vinir said nothing for a moment. Then he gave the slightest of nods.

"I shall see you on the field of battle," he said, then turned on his heel and left, cancelling his father's shielding spell as he went.

I didn't see him for the rest of the day.

You would have thought, with death speeding towards me, the time would have flown. But time felt like glue.

ETERNAL
DRAGGING
STICKINESS
100% vegan

Eons later, I went home to pick up my wand and told my fake family I was going to meet Valerie.

Then I headed to the pavilion where the duel was to happen.

Vinir was already there.

"We meet one last time," said Vinir, and he lifted his wand towards me.

"Very theatrical of you," I said.

"I am no actor," snarled Vinir.

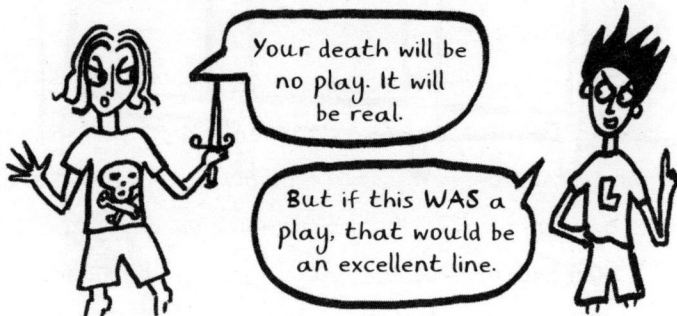

Your death will be no play. It will be real.

But if this WAS a play, that would be an excellent line.

My mind was racing. As the ultimate trickster, I had to think – and fast – of something that would get me out of this situation. All I came up with was to hold him at bay by performing the spell for as long as I could. Even if he was stronger. Even if I knew I could not kill him. Because while I was alive, I could think of an escape plan. Where there's life, there's sneakiness!

Vinir bowed. "May the superior being win," he said and raised his wand higher, throwing a handful of dust into the air. So it began.

When both of us had spoken the words, all that remained was to focus on sucking the life force out of one another. Hyrrokkin had drilled it into me that I needed to clear my mind and focus upon my desire to kill him in order to succeed.

It turned out I had no such desire. What I *did* have was the ability to talk the stone leg off a troll. I have always thought best when I'm talking – so that's what I did.

"This is *not* how I thought I would die," I said. "I was certain it would be an eternal dungeon full of snakes. Or maybe Hyrrokkin would kill me for leaving the toilet seat up."

Yesss, it should be usssss.

"Silence, churl," said Vinir.

Or me.

"I don't really DO silence," I said. "I do words. And, sometimes, pictures."

Your pictures ARE quite good, for someone not an elf.

Your sculptures, on the other hand, are paltry.

"How dare you insult my sculptures!" I said, trying again. "I am not dying with THAT insult unanswered. Your father's not here, so I don't have to hold back for fear of making you look silly in front of him."

But then...

Vinir looked down at his wand. "I was doing this for my father so that he would ... be proud of me. But he is not here. And he will never be proud of me. So why *am* I doing it?"

"I mean..." I felt genuine curiosity. "Why *are* you?"

Vinir leaned against the toilet wall and put his head in his hands. "I don't know. He's not going to respect me. Not ever. So what is the point in trying to impress him?"

I leaned on the wall beside Vinir. "It's pointless. I think he's a total ▓▓▓▓▓▓▓▓▓ ▓▓▓▓▓▓▓▓."

The elf turned and looked at me. "He is, isn't he? But he is my father. My prince! I thought... It felt so right, to avenge my father's honour."

I really thought I was doing the right thing.

I think that a lot. But then it usually turns out I'm not. Being good is really, REALLY complicated.

"I know not what to do." Vinir stood up and started to pace. I believe that he was having a little bit of an elven panic.

"Why don't you come for dinner at our house?" I said, without thinking any of it through.

But why think things through when you can act impulsively on a whim?

In this case, your rashness was kind. !

255

"Heimdall always cooks way too much," I said, ever so casually. I didn't want the proud creature to think I pitied him. I was still frankly terrified of him. But perhaps I understood him ever so slightly now. "His cooking isn't *great*. But it is lots."

"But we are mortal enemies!" said Vinir, with a frown. "No elf would invite an enemy into their home."

"Maybe we don't have to be mortal enemies," I said. "We could be … mortal haters?"

Vinir smiled. "Perhaps we can graduate from deathly enmity to seething hatred, yes. I should like that."

I held out my hand. He shook it.

Done.

When I got home, Hyrrokkin asked where I'd been.

I was about to produce an elaborate web of lies.

But I was just too tired, and I told everyone the truth.

Truth, truth, uncomfortable truth.

"You lied about the duel!" said Heimdall, looking angry enough to buy a new parenting book.

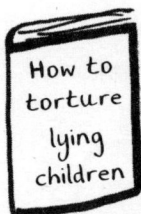

How to torture lying children

"I thought you were up to something," said Hyrrokkin. Her face had an expression that roughly translated as "I am dreaming up punishments beyond your worst nightmares at this very moment".

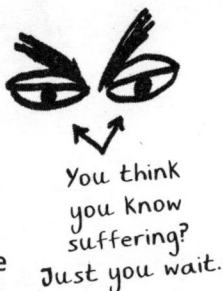

You think you know suffering? Just you wait.

But instead of punishing me on the spot, she demanded assurances from Vinir that the duel was definitely and permanently cancelled.

Forever and a day. This I swear.

257

"Good," said Hyrrokkin, giving me a look that roughly translated as "I am deeply relieved that you are not going to die, but honestly you really do get yourself into some wild situations, and perhaps you should avoid insulting sensitive elves in future".

Hyrrokkin had a VERY expressive face.

I glanced sideways at Vinir, then back at Heimdall and Hyrrokkin.

"The thing is, now his spell on Valerie's mums has lifted, Vinir needs somewhere new to stay," I said. "He's ever-so-slightly banished from Alfheim."

Was he banished for trying to kill my brother?

Vinir blushed and looked at his feet.

"It's a long story," I said. "Tell you later. When I'm not starving. What's for dinner?"

"Given the circumstances, I think we could have a takeaway," said Hyrrokkin. Once the food arrived she said that Vinir could stay with us for now.

"I am *not* sharing my room like some kind of livestock," I said hurriedly.

"You don't have to," said Hyrrokkin. "I have a spell that can create an additional room for the night. Sort of a pocket universe."

I pricked up my ears.

"You are NOT to attempt it," said Hyrrokkin. "You could accidentally bring about Ragnarok, the end of the world."

Did someone say Ragnarok?

Odin appeared with a flash. Seeing Vinir, he raised an eyebrow. "Picking up strays, Heimdall?"

Uh-oh.

Quick, while they're distracted!

"I am not a stray, sire," said Vinir. He stared down Odin with a ferocity that made me extra glad he wasn't trying to kill me any more. "I am an elf lord in exile."

Ah. A fellow wanderer, very good.

"What are you here for, Father?" asked Thor, shyly.

"I merely wish to congratulate you on thwarting the Frost Giants," said Odin. "It's rather nice to visit Earth for a good reason, rather than to witness the chaotic fallout of Loki's antics."

How rude!

! How accurate.

"Thor was VERY brave," I said. Not because I wanted to be nice to Thor, but because Odin was being mean, and due to my contrary nature I have to go against the will of Odin whenever I can without the risk of a pit of snakes.

Sure, Loki.                                                                    !

261

"Vinir helped too," I said, not wanting to look excessively pro-Thor.

Vinir blushed slightly. Honestly, Thor and Vinir are both so NEEDY for praise.

**That's like a mortal crawling through a desert calling someone else thirsty.**

"You have my gratitude," said Odin, and Vinir beamed as though he had been given a great gift.

See, needy!

I waited for Odin to praise me next. He did not. But I did not care in the slightest. I was fine. I was not bothered.

**Lie detected.**

Odin looked at Vinir thoughtfully. "Perhaps, given that you are now an exile, you should stay on Midgard."

Vinir nodded. I wasn't sure if that was a yes, but just in case I needed to get one thing clear.

If he's staying, he's not sharing my room.

262

Odin ignored my very important point.

I shall take my leave. You should sleep soundly in the knowledge that you have prevented an early appearance of Fimbulwinter, the long winter that will usher in Ragnarok.

I wondered if the giants had known what their plan would lead to. Or were they so focused on creating their own chilly paradise on Earth that they did not think about what might come next? Did the Frost Giants even know about the prophecy of Ragnarok?

Many interesting questions! Well, they were a bit interesting – interesting enough for me to think about it for a full five minutes before getting distracted by something more compelling: what might be for pudding?

There's no fruit because someone used it for a spell. But ... cake?

I suppose I can cope with this sad substitute.

After dinner I was about to make my way upstairs when Hyrrokkin and Heimdall stopped me. They looked serious. Never a good thing.

But instead of giving me some terrible punishment, they both gave me a hug in turn.

"You did really well," said Hyrrokkin.

"We're proud of you, Loki," said Heimdall.

And – Diary, you will detect no lies in this – I didn't care any more about the praise of Odin. Not a bit.

> ! Truth detected indeed. I'm proud of you, too, Loki.

Shhh, you're going to make me weepy before bed!

# Day Thirty:
## Wednesday

### LOKI VIRTUE SCORE OR LVS:

# 0

**400 points gained for making peace with Vinir! I won't even have to reset your score for a fresh start next month!**

At breakfast club, I sat with Valerie and Georgina. I explained that Vinir might be staying around, and how Odin came to Earth specifically to praise me.

I am sometimes astounded by your ability to lie to yourself.

!

"After Vinir and Sif, I'm starting to wonder if half the children in town are secretly ancient beings in disguise," said Georgina, looking around at the other mortal children in the breakfast club.

"I'm not one," said Valerie. "I am definitely human."

"Are you SURE you're not secretly an elf princess?" asked Georgina. "You can tell me."

Look, round ears!

"Fine, I believe you. Mostly." Then Georgina turned to me. "So, he definitely called off the duel for ever?"

It was inevitable, really, given how charming I am.

When both girls had stopped laughing, I told them the whole story – including the fact that I'd lied about calling off the duel.

Georgina said, "Well, I'm glad he's not going to kill you."

"Aha!" I said, stabbing at the air with my finger in a gesture of pure triumph. "You clearly love me and we are officially best friends now and you've forgiven me?"

"I feel like you still have a lot to learn about friendship," said Georgina, "if not wanting someone to die means you're best friends."

I sighed. Mortal friendship truly WAS an onerous and tedious maze of unknown complexities.

"But Loki?" she said, leaning closer so she could use my real name without anyone overhearing.

I flinched, in case she was going to do something violent to me.

267

"No need to get sappy," said Georgina, giving me a playful shove. But it was that shove that made me realize she really HAD forgiven me. It was the kind of play-fighting she usually reserved for Valerie.

So, I'd begun the month with two enemies and now I have none. Unless you count some of the larger bully children. And the PE teacher. And the giants, obviously. But still.

I am calling that a WIN.

TO BE
CONTINUED...

# Acknowledgements

Thanks to all the gods and heroes at Walker, from the mighty sales team to the cunning language-shifting tricksters in rights, the magical production team and the marvels of mythical proportions in marketing and publicity.

**KAREN LAWLER**... The Best Wife for All Eternity

**MOLLY KER HAWN**... Agent of Asgard

**NON PRATT**... Word God

**LINDSAY WARREN**... Word God Over the Water

**JAMIE HAMMOND**... Art God

**KIRSTEN COZENS**... She of the Publicity Pantheon

**KAREN COEMAN**... Vampire Goddess

**RACHEL FATUROTI**... Comics God

**KATHERINE BEARD**... Keeper of the runes

**SAMANTHA-LOUISE HAYDEN**... God of
wisdom

**TEAM SWAG**... HORSE!

**FEMINISM 2.0**... Gods of deep thought

**ALICE, HELENA AND VICKY**... Mighty
Valkyries

**DEE AND ROBIN**... Gods of London

**ABBIE AND ELIZABETH**... Pocket Gods

**EMMY WOODS**... Insult consultant